Almost Whole

Almost Whole

Kopal Khanna

PARTRIDGE
A Penguin Random House Company

ISBN:	Softcover	978-1-4828-3969-2
	eBook	978-1-4828-3968-5

To order additional copies of this book, contact
Partridge India
000 800 10062 62
orders.india@partridgepublishing.com

www.partridgepublishing.com/india

To Papa, Maa and Di...for many reasons.

"You create your own universe as you go along"
– Winston Churchill

ACKNOWLEDGEMENT

I would take this opportunity to thank all members of the non-profit organization – Meena - *Sanatkada Samajik Pahel* – for inspiring me without even knowing it. This one is for the women inmates in the Jail, who offered me a biscuit every time I met them, even though they were hungry themselves. This one is for their kids, who asked me questions I never had the right answers to.

I also extend my gratitude towards Vatsala Srivastava, who helped me edit the final draft of the book in a relatively short time period.

Lastly, I am grateful to Pooja Anna Pant for designing a cover that sums up the text beautifully.

AUTHOR'S NOTE

The author interned with a non-profit for a period of three months wherein she went to the Jail thrice a week and taught the women inmates English, Hindi and Mathematics. This story is set against that backdrop.

However, this is a work of fiction; none of the characters and incidents mentioned in this book is real, though actual people and true stories have inspired most of them. Part of the author's conversations with the inmates have been highlighted but not with precision. The author is not the protagonist.

TONIGHT when I look at the stars, I just know there is something different about them. *Wondulful!* She would surely have whispered, gazing straight into the cosmos while trying hard to avoid any eye contact with me, knowing that she had unknowingly made the same mistake again. Certain emotions linger on and they feel like the tapering sound of a wind chime. Not too prominent, but still there. Not loud enough to distract you but audible enough to constantly make you feel its presence. My story is about this sound, this sound that feels like it will perish any minute, but sooner or later you realize that it is a constant, the only thing worth perishing for.

"Still searching?" Someone standing right behind me asked. I must have forgotten to lock the door again. The voice was familiar, not the kind you automatically associate with a face but the kind that doesn't need a face, a voice having its own identity sort of logic. I heard, but chose not to respond. The stillness of that moment was too beautiful to be destroyed by a question that could have been answered without spoken words.

"*Maa* called," the voice spoke again after half a minute of silence, silence that was mellifluous on my part, and probably uneasy on his.

"It's been really long, Ayanna. Let's go home?"

Really long. The concept of Time has always amused me. How does one decide if it's been really long or if we have travelled just a few miles? It's funny how humans think of the universe as their home, how they forget that if we ever try to trace the history of our planets, the stars or the galaxies, we'll be caught up in a story that would take us a billion years in reverse. I wanted to tell him this but it would have been too much of an effort, and that too a futile one.

"I know, but I am not ready to give up yet," I said finally, still staring at infinity from the small window in my room and added "...nor will I ever be" to my statement, after a little pause.

"I am staying on the 2nd floor, room number 24." He informed.

I was too lost in my own story, I could see glimpses of those forty days right in front of my eyes, there was no room for any other thought.

"I am not ready to give up yet," he reiterated, and I could hear the sound of his footsteps steadily walking away from me. He stopped for a while and supplemented, "nor will I ever be," and shut the door with a thud.

PART 1

Flashback: 2010

"I was fourteen then: it had been exactly nine years and Sitara had been closer to me than anyone else in my family of seven people. It was Sitara's ninth birthday that day. Like every year I had baked his favorite chocolate cupcakes and had neatly placed them in a container that looked like it had been custom-made to hold my nine small spheres of mouth-watering chocolate. I placed one candle on each cupcake, carefully picking the brightest colors so that they were in perfect contrast with the dark, dull color the cocoa beans had given to my chocolate icing. Our emotions make us act in funny ways, they drain out all the logic, pragmatism and everything similar that would prevent you from looking foolish. I'd ceremoniously do this year after year, just to ultimately blow the candles myself and see half eaten bits of my cupcakes lying all over the house waiting for their turn to enter the trash can.

"I'd love to describe him to you, Kali. I haven't spoken about him since that day. But you, you just made all my walls collapse, one by one, without even realizing what you were doing."

Innocence, I thought, although rare was the most beautiful attribute in a person. I remember not being able to decide whether it was its rarity that made it beautiful or its beauty that made it rare. So much time had passed but everything was etched in my soul so flawlessly that even though everybody thought it would fade away with time, I knew it wouldn't. Ever.

"Walls are meant to protect a house, right? Did your walls protect you?" She asked me, lying down next to me on the thin mattress, which often made me think if sleeping on the floor would be any better.

"At least I thought so." I replied, catching a quick glimpse of her face that was staring curiously at the night sky.

She suddenly got up in complete bewilderment, "That means I did a bad thing by breaking your walls?"

"No, the best thing anyone could do," I remarked without thinking twice.

It was true. I don't remember being lonely in life, nor do I remember being sad for a long period of time, but I remember feeling empty sometimes. The kind of emptiness that occupies the maximum space. The feeling which is insignificant to others, but to you, it determines your life, whether you want it to or not.

"Save your questions for the end. Now, do you want to know what Sitara looked like or not?" This was my favorite way of bringing her never-ending cycle of queries to an end, by giving her more matter to think about, starting a fresh cycle of questions soon.

"He had the most serene yet eager pair of eyes I had ever seen. I would intentionally avoid eye contact with him when he demanded something irrational, like the box of doughnuts my dad would bring for me and my sister, Rihanna, every Sunday, because it became impossible to break his heart after looking into his eyes. Believe me Kali; you would have loved him, exactly like I did. He wasn't particularly furry but he had curly golden hair, and his ears were always in attention mode, except when he demanded love or was plain lazy. I wouldn't call him miniature but he wasn't too tall either."

"How tall? Bigger than me?" Kali asked enthusiastically, her eyes wide open with excitement and fear.

"Um, if he stood on his hind feet, he would easily be able to lick your nose." I imagined first and then spoke.

"My parents gifted him to me on my sixth birthday, the best gift I could have asked for. I would spend my entire day with him. He slept in my room, ate from my plate and shared my favorite ice cream, something I had never even done with Nadiya, my best friend from school. I told him my deepest secrets, took him for walks and played fetch with him. He would play with me in my dollhouse, be happy when I was happy and unhappy when my mother yelled at me. He'd even barked at her when it got a little too much. He was a true friend."

"Did he talk to you?" Kali asked quickly. I am now sure she was trying to point out that she was the better friend. If

I had realized this back then I would have probably chosen my next words more carefully.

"He listened and I needed that the most," I told her without putting in much thought.

"Oh," she sighed. "What happened to him?" She added, still not being able to let go of my favorite habit of hers.

"The inevitable."

I remember my eyes getting wet then, not in a dramatic way, but subtly, such that even Kali didn't come to know about it. It was my grief and only I could feel it completely, even though at that point of time it was being shared for the first time in ten years. That is the thing about sorrow; it is never small enough for you and never big enough for the other person. Maybe this was the thought behind not speaking to anyone about the darker side all my life. Strangely, that day the emotions were flowing without any barriers; they were like wild horses, exactly like they were meant to be. I used the word 'inevitable' to console myself probably. We humans always try to find ways to escape what is hard for us to accept; the most common escape is to blame the creator, or God as some may choose to call him. It is hilarious how what we believe in depends on our convenience.

"Almost the entire family had gathered to witness the annual cake cutting ceremony," I continued. "I would hold Sitara in my hands and somehow manage to hold a knife in the same hands too. Rihanna and I would blow the candles and leave the cupcakes at Sitara's mercy while everyone sang the birthday song for him."

"How was his ninth birthday different from all the others?" Kali asked.

"It was his last," I answered.

"We were playing fetch-the-ball near our outhouse like every other day - Rihanna, Adi, Sitara and me, when suddenly, Adi threw the ball too high and it jumped over the fence and as we had assumed then, landed on the other side of the road. The four of us went running to the main gate to assure the ball was still within our reach."

Most people get sick of monotony, but the truth is that often when this monotony breaks, it causes a lot of damage. We constantly crave for change, and when change finally hits us, we realize we want to crawl back to monotony.

"Sitara, as always, came running behind us speedily, wagging his tail with full velocity. When Rihanna went to pick up the ball from across the road, Sitara followed and I let him. I hadn't even taken my eyes off Sitara when I heard the sound of a speeding bus, darting towards my sister and my only companion. I still remember the color of that bus, Kali. Blue with a thick white line running around its edges. I wasn't even given a full second to give the most important decision of my life a thought. Rihanna or Sitara? I ran in blind faith, screaming out Sitara's name and pushing Rihanna towards Adi. I had expected Sitara to come running towards me, like he always had, except, he did not. The bus run him over, its heavy tyres had crushed my soul into the tiniest of pieces. The sound of his last screech still echoes in my ears sometimes, mostly when I am about to fall asleep."

"Do you feel like you should have saved Sitara instead?" This was Kali's next question.

We can live a lifetime hiding the biggest truths about ourselves, often times from ourselves. Nobody had ever asked me this question before, probably because everyone assumed it was a stupid question. Who would choose a dog over a sister?

"Yes." I said.

"Then why didn't you?" She asked like one asks questions with the easiest of answers.

I remember telling her something about how blood ties take precedence over all the other bonds we make on this earth, no matter what they mean to us.

To which she commented, "What if that person is the only person who makes you truly happy?" I didn't have an answer to her question then, but if I ever meet her again, I'll know what to say.

"Kali, I spent days and months weeping. My family and acquaintances were so proud of me because Adi and Ri had told everyone about my act of bravery. Honestly, I hadn't done anything more cowardly ever. I blamed myself every day. I wish I had someone to share my guilt with. If I had told my mother about it, she would have scolded me for harboring such thoughts. I let time do its magical healing. Slowly the memories got blurred and I got occupied with my everyday activities, but some days I'd miss him too much, and those days I could literally feel my chest getting heavy."

"Do you still have those days?" She spoke after taking a sip of water from my glass.

"Not often, but yes." I told her.

"Don't blame yourself for his death, *Ummi*. I think you did the right thing. You broke your own heart but saved a lot of hearts from breaking."

I smiled, ruffled her hair and assumed, "I think that is what made my heart ache a little less, my *Noor*."

II

"Will I ever get out of this place?" She solicited. Future tense. Uncertainty.

What do I tell a 12 year old that has been in Jail since the past two years because her own mother murdered her father? How do I instill hope in her life? Where do I find sunshine in the dark? I recollect questioning myself when Kali first asked me this question.

"Can I call you *Ummi*?" She asked before I could come up with a convincing response for her previous question.

Muslims call their mothers *Ammi*, I thought. I wasn't sure if I was ready to be addressed by that name, or rather, if I was responsible enough.

Someone or the other had always been there to take care of me all my life, and that day someone expected me to do the same.

"*Ummi... Umeed*," she elucidated.

I looked at her with something I today recognize as adoration and tenderness.

"Why would you call me *Umeed*?"

"I feel like you are my *Umeed*, my hope. I trust you to make things right."

I pecked her forehead and I remember feeling something change inside me. Today I know that that was the change I had been longing for, the change that had made me travel a thousand miles away from home, towards a home.

"You are my *Noor*, the light of my life." I embraced her first and told this to her later.

III

If I had to sit down and describe what Kali looked like, I'd avoid it at first for I fear she would come across as someone very ordinary to the listener. But of course, if I absolutely had to tell a person I would choose to describe the way she appeared to me when I first met her.

I had been in the prison for two entire days. If I could find words to describe how I felt back then, my pen would write them down, but our language hasn't reached where our emotions have and hence certain emotions can't be written down, they can merely be felt.

I was walking towards my room, *barric* as they called it there, probably a short form for 'barricade,' which would denote some sort of a barrier or obstruction, after failing to get through to my family for the fifth time. I felt so smothered; I could literally feel the lack of fresh air around me. It was more mental that physical though. The warden had allowed me three extra calls in the last 48 hours but my ill fate, or so I thought at that time, made sure that all the numbers I tried were not reachable. The thought of being stuck within the four walls of the 'Mahila Niketan Jail', miles away from my home in London, for the rest of my life took away whatever little strength I had left within me.

I was about to cross the fine line between hopefulness and hopelessness when I heard someone scream "*Didi!*" I looked behind to check if somebody was addressing me by that name, though not until that person had called out

"*Didi!*" four times. I had dodged any sort of conversation with the inmates for the past two days. Although I call myself a social person, who could make friends within minutes, I did not feel the need to build any sort of relationships here, because, firstly, I wasn't there to stay, and secondly, for the first time in my life I felt intimidated by everyone around me. They were prisoners. Criminals. Murderers. Thieves. Kidnappers. Outlaws. It was only later that I realized that I was a prisoner too but not a criminal.

When I turned I saw a little girl, aged ten maybe, running barefoot toward me in full speed. She wore a deep purple knee length frock with white frilly edges. Her black hair seemed to have been cut short sloppily but when she halted in front of me I realized she had uneven fringes that covered her forehead. These fringes gave her an appearance that made me ponder if she had ever looked any different. However, I couldn't come up with any alternatives that better suited her face. She was exactly half my size and to make the picture a little clearer, I boast about being almost a six-footer. Her skin could undoubtedly be classified as dusky, maybe not naturally, but due to excessive exposure to sunlight. Though the scar running across her right cheek was the most noticeable thing on her face, somehow I could only concentrate on her big grey eyes glaring at me while she stood in front of me, breathless, with my earring placed exactly in the middle of her tiny palm that she somehow managed to raise to the level of my shoulders.

"I think it fell off your ears. Here, keep it." She said in the most beautiful sounding voice I had ever heard. She spoke in Hindi. I had been born and brought up in London and that was my first visit to India, a country I had heard so much about from my grandmother. I literally grew up hearing stories about this place that would have been my homeland if my parents hadn't decided to settle down in England after their marriage.

I remember my grandmother, who passed away three months before I landed in India, telling me, "*Nanni jaan* (Little darling), that country has given me everything that is precious to me, I miss it dearly. I wish you and Rihanna could go there sometime. I promise you, you'll learn the best lessons of your life there, and if you are even a little lucky, you'll make relationships that will live on forever in your heart."

"Thank you, little one! I must have been really lost." I informed her and picked up the earring from her small mud-spattered hands.

I just couldn't manage to look beyond her eyes. I felt like someone had cast a spell on me.

"You came two days back, *didi*?" She asked enthusiastically, as if she had found a new friend to play with.

My response was a gloomy nod and I did manage to finally take my eyes off the little grey in her eyes.

"Why are you here? Do you know English? Did you kill someone?" Her excitement could be felt in her voice.

I was a little taken aback. I remember standing there expressionless.

"Why are you here?" She repeated.

"Maybe because there is nobody who can get me out of here" I sighed.

"Even your family doesn't want you anymore?" She questioned casually.

"Why would you ask me that? What are you doing in this Jail?" I asked. I took a good ten minutes to ask the question that I should have asked first; what the hell was a child doing in that place?

"Oh, my mother killed my father and since there was nobody else to take care of me, I was asked to stay in the Jail with her. I am here because there is nobody who is willing to get me out of here." She stated.

I remember feeling a chill run down my spine. She had just told me about the harshest reality of her life so causally that I couldn't even make out if she was just pretending to be fine or whether she was actually happy in this confinement. I had spend all these years trying to hide the little hurts, the small failures, the little guilt's because I never wanted to sound vulnerable or weak, because I felt the need to trust a person completely before telling him about my deepest secrets. And here she was, this little girl, telling me the biggest truth of her life with a smile on her face.

I couldn't do much then. I had always been emotionally retarded. All I could manage then was an embrace; I wasn't sure though, if she needed that hug or not, but one thing I knew for sure was that I needed it.

I held her tight for two minutes till she decided to let go.

"I am not unhappy. I just miss my old school sometimes." She informed while trying to remove the mud that was stuck in her fingernails.

That was the first thing I had learnt from her; you don't need to hide your deepest secrets from anyone because they define you and if you keep hiding them, it leaves room for false assumptions. I had assumed she was fragile while surprisingly she was stronger than most of the people I had met.

After talking to her for another half-an-hour I found out that her name was Kali, and that she was 12 years old. She belonged to some small town named *Golaganj* nearby and lived with her parents. Her father was an aggressive short-tempered auto driver, who would beat up her mother and her every night after he got home. One day, her father hit her with a glass rod, which cut through her right cheek; her mother couldn't resist anymore and pitilessly killed her own husband with the same glass rod. Later, their neighbors, who according to her were always nagging, took her mother to the police station and got her arrested. Her mother didn't speak a word in her defense and readily surrendered. According to the judge she had to serve 14 years in Jail, out of which they had completed two. She told me she loved her mother a lot, not because she protected her from her father, but because she taught her how to stand by whatever you do, no matter how bad it is, since in that moment it was the best you could do.

She narrated her story to me with such ease, like she was singing a song. I had read similar stories in books and newspapers or seen such people in a couple of movies but this was for real. I had just met somebody living this life. I felt so heavy I couldn't move or speak.

We humans get so involved with ourselves that we become oblivious to the lives of others. We are so caught up in our own little world that we forget we are a part of something bigger, something deeper.

"Will you teach me English? It is not like I don't know it at all, I am in class four and I can say '*Elephunt*'." She boasted.

"That is wonderful, Kali. Yes of course I'll teach you English." I patted her back while saying this.

"*Wondulful!*" She said.

"*One-dur.*" I corrected.

"*One-dul.*" She recapped.

"Um, it is the sound of 'r' and not 'l'," I explained.

"You mean 'l'," she said.

After repeating this exercise many times, even with different words that had the same sound, like rubber, eraser, I realized that she couldn't differentiate between the sound of 'r' and 'l'. I found this very adorable but was still adamant to make her learn the right thing. In those two hours I became so involved in her world that I forgot everything about my own. Hardly had I realized back then that her world would change mine completely. I understand now that the beauty of life lies in these connections, this invisible force that binds all humanity. It is funny how the same gravitational force keeps all of us rooted to the ground, yet we all see ourselves as different from others. How we forget that if it weren't for this similarity, we'd all merely be rootless floating objects and nothing else.

We were in the middle of discussing how water is our favorite element on earth when the bell rang. She said, "I like water because of its color. *Ammi* keeps telling me it doesn't have a color, but it does, we can see water, can't we?" I told her I liked it because of its quality to take the shape of any container it is poured in. She laughed when I said that. The bell, which rang everyday exactly at 3:OO in the afternoon, indicated that it was time to have lunch. I hadn't had lunch in the last two days. I told myself that the food looked unhygienic but I guess the real reason was that somewhere deep down I was hoping I would get attention and sympathy. However, soon I realized there was no room for these two words here and that I had to take care of myself.

"Are you hungry? Let's go eat?" I asked her.

"If I don't eat now, I won't get food till 7:30. I am always hungry when this bell rings."

It was true I realized. I believe it becomes a part of your system after a while; your body starts functioning according to these rules. It is not like home, where food is always available and there is someone or the other always requesting you to eat it. Over here, you need to leave whatever you are doing at 3:00 everyday because if you don't, you stay hungry till 7:30 and nobody cares. I was quick to learn this, and I'd thank Kali for that. On asking she also informed me that they serve boiled rice, yellow *daal* and boiled potato six days a week, and on Saturdays they served beans and *daal* instead. The food looked and tasted identical everyday, which sometimes made the inmates feel as if large amounts of food had been cooked in one go and preserved somewhere. On special occasions like Independence Day and New Year, they were given a dessert with the food. Kali wasn't too fond of the kind of dessert they offered and wished they had served her favorite chocolate ice cream instead.

I had spent two days in that Jail and had almost lost the hope of ever eating my favorite ice cream again and here she was, this little girl, hoping to get her favorite chocolate ice cream after two years of eating boiled rice and *daal* everyday for lunch.

So, this was the first time I met Kali and also the first time I felt like I could hold on, that I could manage a laugh in captivity, that I wasn't all about freedom and travel and that maybe a part of me yearned to find happiness in just one place. After that day, as promised, I had to teach Kali English and so we would sit together every night after the *barrics* were locked. We would study less and talk more and although I was the teacher, she would unknowingly teach me things that I'd remember for a lifetime.

IV

The prison was nothing like I had imagined it to be. We form these blurred images of things we haven't seen yet because that is how our mind works. We quickly paint pictures in our head and often end up seeing something completely different when we actually reach the place. When the police van was taking me to the Central Jail, which was about 20 kilometers away from the main city, I just kept thinking about what jail would be like. I imagined brutal, filthy criminals behind massive iron bars, a small unkempt campus where women convicts would be working endlessly, tied to chains and probably supervised by a staff member, who would scream at them and often beat them up when they wouldn't do their jobs properly. However, what I saw was completely unusual; the Jail was spread across a vast area and had a lot of open space around it. From the outside it seemed like a college campus if you hadn't already read the enormous front hoarding, which announced 'Mahila Niketan Jail.' The path leading to the main black gate was surrounded by trees on both sides and had been kept clean and tidy. The gate was opened only when the constables showed the letter from the officer. After all the formalities had been completed, and I had been assigned my *barric* and my week's duties, the warden guided me to my cell. Strangely, the people seemed nice and helpful contrary to what I had thought. Probably they knew that I had been caught in a trap and would be stuck in there for sometime.

Inside, instead of small narrow rooms, all I saw was open space. There was a large hospital to my left and a big hall to my right. After walking for five minutes we entered the core area of the Jail. I could see a total of seven *barrics.* The women were all dressed in colorful saris and suits, unlike the black and white garments I thought they'd be wearing, and didn't look like criminals at all. I was too scared to even look at them for more than a second though. The warden took me to *barric* number 3 and left after arranging a mattress for me. My *barric* was as big as a basketball court and was shared by around twenty women. This I assumed after looking at the number of mattresses spread on the floor. There was no way to get out of the four walls except the huge iron gate, which must be locked most of the times I thought. There was a tiny window on the front wall through which I could see the sky. Although I didn't know it then, that would be my solace for a long time.

"What's your name?" A woman seated next to my mattress asked. I was too emotionally and physically drained to say anything and so I ran outside my *barric* and just cried for hours.

That is how I was welcomed to this place. Unceremoniously and abruptly. That was the first of the many days, which would change my life completely.

V

You know that feeling when you suddenly find a mission in life, when all of a sudden you realize there is so much left to learn and do. I found my mission in Kali. This mission wasn't to teach her English and make her eligible for a better future but to make myself more suitable for the world outside those four walls, literal four walls. I had always loved, lived, laughed and had assumed I was a happy person without even knowing happiness. I was close to many people but would maintain a measured distance between them and my core. I had experienced pleasure; both physical and emotional. But some days, some very rare days I would think about life while bathing, and would scribble on the mist formed on the glass of the shower cubicle with my index finger, and surprisingly I would always end up writing, '*almost whole.*' I never thought about it much though, because life outside that shower cubicle was very fast. I was always a very strong-headed person; I did what I wanted to do, when I wanted to do it. I loved almost fully and cared with all my heart. I was almost always too scared of falling freely though, I made sure I had strapped myself well before jumping. This doesn't mean I wasn't attached to people or things, only that I could detach without much difficulty. Or so I thought. The reason being: nobody had ever seen my core, and strangely

I hadn't seen it often either. It wasn't like I didn't want to; I would often feel a very strong urge to face it, to show it, but that feeling was never prominent enough and hence I thought it wasn't important. Kali, a 12 year old little child, showed me how this core was important. She had learnt what I was unable to in 24 years. That is why I wanted to stay, till whenever I could, in this confinement. It made me feel freer than ever.

On one of our star gazing nights she asked me, "Whom do you love the most in this world?"

To my surprise I did not have an answer, I did not know that one person I could die for. Nobody asks us these questions usually; hence we never feel the need to know these things. But strangely, even after thinking very hard, I couldn't come up with an answer. I could see a collage of people in front me, everyone who loved me more than I deserved and all the people I loved but I couldn't see that one person, standing above all, whom I had loved the most, with every little part of me. I was a little disappointed with myself and so was Kali when I said, "I love a lot of people, there are too many."

"The most, *Ummi*, THE MOST," she stressed.

"I don't know, my love, never thought about it," I said.

"Why do you need to think about it? You just get to know. I know." She told me.

"Whom do you love the most then?" I asked her, hoping that she wouldn't notice I hadn't answered her question.

"My little brother," she told me without even thinking for a second.

"Really? That's amazing Kali! Where is he? Why doesn't he stay with you here?"

"He died when he was six years old. Mum tells me he touched the wrong wire while trying to turn on a lamp. It has been 3 years. I hate lamps."

I looked for her hand and held it softly.

"It is very saddening. I can't be with him all the time. He was my companion; I would never feel the need to have anyone else when he was around. *Ammi* thinks I have forgotten him because I don't speak about him much, but I feel him around me all the time. I could do anything to get him back; I'll make sure I destroy all the lamps in the world before that. I don't cry when I miss him, I know he can't come back and I am okay with that but he is still that person I love the most. He is still that person I share everything with." She told me while holding my hand securely.

"You don't feel the need to have another companion?" I asked gently.

"It's hard, but I hope I do find one." she answered.

Till that day I had thought that to move on was the most essential lesson life teaches us. But I was wrong. The most important lesson was to hold on, to accept, and to be able to hope. I had spent so much time trying to recover from hurts, trying to forget a love, to get over a failure, to forget a betrayal, it was like I was in a dark den and could do nothing while I was in it. That day Kali taught me how that dark den was the most important part of my life, how the time spent in that dark den decides who I will be once I could see the light again.

VI

"What does it look like *Ummi*? The place where you come from?" Kali asked me while looking at the stars. She would never look at me while talking, although I really wished she did.

"It is beautiful! It has a river, huge buildings, lush green parks, the busiest streets, the quietest places, so much history and a promising future. Oh and yummy ice cream too." I paused for a little after saying that, just to look at Kali's reaction but she was in deep thought as if she was visualizing what I was saying. "It has love and also loneliness, it has success and also failures. It is the only place I can live in."

"Even my city is just like that, *Ummi*. I swear." I smiled at her and nodded without saying a word.

"How far is it from here?"

"Really far away, my love. You'll have to fly to get there."

"You mean take an airplane?" I would always feel so silly after treating her like a little child, always forgetting how she was wiser than me.

I laughed idiotically and said, "yes."

"Have you ever lived anywhere else?"

"No, why?"

"How do you know then?"

"Know what?"

"That that's the only place where you can live?"

She was right. We often tend to get too attached to certain places or things and fail to imagine our world without them but sooner or later we do forfeit these things either by choice or because of circumstances, and realize that we are doing very well without them.

“That’s true. It’s the only place I’ve lived in and maybe that’s why I assumed it’s the only place I can live in.” I said.

“You know we are all made from stars.” I finally spoke after five minutes of unusual silence. With Kali around, there was never a moment of muteness but that day she seemed to be relatively quiet.

“How? You mean to say when we make a wish upon the stars we are truly talking to ourselves?” She would always come up with ways to question my logical, scientifically proven statements and I would always feel how narrow our perspectives actually are.

“Maybe.” I replied because I couldn’t think of anything better.

“Maybe? Tell me please,” she insisted.

Initially I thought of explaining the entire concept of stardust and how we were born only after millions and millions of stars died several years ago, but wasn’t that too saddening for someone who loved stars? Her thought process was so much better than mine. We all were nothing but stars.

“You know shooting stars, right? You ask them for something and it is believed that the wish comes true sooner or later. Kali, that star is in front of us for a few seconds. It is falling; we know that it will disappear and we also know that we have just those few seconds to make a wish. And sometimes, not often but sometimes we realize our greatest wish in those few seconds. The falling stars don’t fulfill wishes; they do us a bigger favor by making us realize what we are truly wishing for.” I tried explaining. I remember feeling happy about myself back then. So often it happens that you realize you knew something only after you say it out loud. So from that day I made sure I said things out loud.

"I have never seen a shooting star though," she said with a frown. She never frowned otherwise.

I suddenly got up from the mattress and asked her, "You know your wish?"

"I want to see the place where you come from," she said with the most innocent smile on her face.

"Me too Kali, I want to see that place from your eyes too." I caressed her hair gently while saying this.

VII

"Nadiya and I were best friends till high school, after which we gradually lost touch. Her parents had decided to move to California because her father got a lucrative job there. It is funny Kali, how money is driving the world mad. It didn't take them any time to make this decision. I found this idea really upsetting back then, that I had to sacrifice my best friend because her parents wanted a little more money. I was so furious. I went to talk to her parents one day and told them they had no right to take away my best friend from me. They treated me like a little child and tried to bribe me with the idea of sending gifts and cookies from California. I didn't even make any farewell gifts for Nadiya, you know. I was so mad at her and everyone." I was telling her about another chapter of my life that day.

"So, did you find a new best friend after she left?" Kali questioned.

"No. And it wasn't because I missed her too much or she was irreplaceable. It was because Nadiya's moving out and getting too busy with life and making new friends in California had left me a little scarred. I didn't want another best friend who would just walk out of my life and give me a week's notice before doing so. I realize only now that I won't always get to pick, I don't get to choose and that sometimes others will choose for me and leave me with no choice." I told her.

"But it wasn't like I didn't come close to people. I made better friends. And I even forgot about Nadiya slowly but I never called anyone my 'best friend' again."

"Why were you always so scared of getting hurt?" She asked me.

"I wasn't. I just felt the need to protect myself well."

"That's silly. You are protecting yourself from the best things in life."

"I guess you are right."

"I am. It is silly to say you enjoy the rain when you pick up an umbrella every time you leave your house just because the weather forecast says it will rain."

"But that's also clever, isn't it?"

"No. You can't say you want to live fully and still walk so carefully all the time."

"How do you know all this?"

"I've noticed."

I ruffled her hair again and smiled.

VIII

On one of those nights when I really missed home and felt absolutely clueless about where my life was going, Kali surprised me with a small card she had made for me during her school hours. She used to go to "Balika Mandir Government School," which was very close to the Jail. She had to leave her previous, better school and join this one because the government allowed the dependent children in the Jail to go to only some specific schools. She learnt Hindi, Mathematics and Science there and was definitely the brightest in her class. She enjoyed learning more than anything.

"I am not a very good artist, but here, I made this for you." She held an A4 size dark blue colored sheet in her hand.

"This is so sweet of you, my love," I said taking the sheet of paper from her hands.

The side, which I could see, had a tiny heart colored in red made on the bottom right hand of the page. When I flipped the sheet to look at the other side I saw the most thoughtful piece of art somebody had ever made for me. I knew I would keep it close to my heart for a very long time. The upper half of the page had been very carefully filled with silver sparkle that represented the night sky. On the lower half were two matchstick figures, one small and the other exactly double of the first one, lying down on a grey mattress. It was so beautiful; I could almost feel the moment.

"You are a wonderful artist Kali. This is the best card ever." I told her after pecking her forehead.

And in that moment I forgot about home, my situation and the unknown.

"That's you and me," she explained.

"Yes, I know, that's us." I told her.

"My teacher asked me to make something for someone who is very important to me."

"Why didn't you make one for your mother, *Noor*?"

"She is the most important, that's true, but she doesn't understand this kind of love; the one we show through cards and presents; she doesn't need it."

"What made you think I understood it?"

"I wanted to try."

"So, what do you think?"

"It made you smile."

"Sure it did," I agreed.

Kali was really pleased to see that I liked what she had made for me. That night I remember being particularly tired though. I had had a long day. As usual I hadn't heard anything from the jail or the superintendent and my frustration was beginning to smother me. Honestly, it wasn't that I was unhappy or that the conditions were too ruthless for survival but it was the uncertainty that killed me. The fact that I didn't know how long this would last. Not just the discomforts of my life in Jail but also the strange peace I felt in this captivity. I didn't know anything. Nobody was willing to tell me anything. It was funny how a part of me actually wanted to stay.

"You'll leave me soon no?"

"If I had a choice Kali, I'd keep you with me forever."

"But you don't have a choice?"

"I do. You come with me to London?"

"I can't leave my mother alone here. You stay."

"That's not possible, *Noor.* It's been a full month and now my family must be very worried about me. I have a mother too no."

"But you said you liked it with me."

"I love it with you around. I want you. I want to keep you. I want to take you along."

"I want you too. But what will happen to my mother? I can't leave her like that."

"You are the best daughter in the world Kali, and the best in general. You've made the right decision."

"I'll miss you a lot."

"I am not even leaving yet. I don't know when will I leave, but whenever I do, I'll give you this choice again, of coming home with me, and then you can make your final decision."

"*Wondulful!*" She exclaimed and then we looked at each other and started laughing as if this was our inside joke now.

IX

"Why did you come here?" She asked me after we had had a long conversation about all the places I had travelled to.

"I can't say."

"What do you mean?"

"I mean there is no one reason."

"Maybe you could tell me the most important one then?"

"All the reasons are important."

"Then tell me all. I am not even sleepy yet."

"Today is the 13th right? My grandmother passed away exactly four months ago. I was not particularly close to her but we would talk sometimes. She had played a major role in my upbringing and although we were intimate till my early teens, we gradually fell apart. All our conversations revolved around India, her homeland, and how this country gave her everything she can call her own. She was a beautiful old lady. I can't even imagine what she looked like in her prime but at 83 her face had the perfect glow. She had long brown hair that she'd never leave untied and her eyes, flawlessly lined with mascara all the time, were so full of life and wisdom. Her husband, my granddad died when she was 65 and she missed him dearly. Her second favorite topic of discussion was her priceless love life. I know I am drifting away from the topic a little but I wish to talk about her some more. This will also help you understand my decision. She'd always tell me stories about how she was a great actor and would participate in her college plays. She had always wanted to become an actress secretly. You know there is so much beauty within everyone. I wonder why don't people realize it. Maybe since we are unable to step into their shoes because we are too busy trying to fit in our own first. How does one understand someone else if he is still struggling to understand oneself? I really tried hard to picture my grandma like she described herself in her early days but failed mostly. She would tell me all sorts of stories, about her crushes, her huge house in Lucknow - a small town in India, her cousins, her neighbors, her career as a teacher and what not. Of course most of these stories became hazy in my mind as I grew up but I remember one very clearly and that one just kept crossing my mind when grandma was on her deathbed. She once told me about how when she was nineteen she was so full of life that she hated the idea of death, the idea of breathing towards your own end. She didn't want to be sick and miserable and ultimately die. She thought about this for months and months till when one day she finally realized the thought behind the concept of death. She had gone out of town to attend a relative's wedding for four days. The house had a television set, which was a rarity in those days. She loved watching TV and told me how she even missed two ceremonies because she was glued to the set. Even after her mother yelled at her several times she didn't stop, until finally on the third day the television wire had to be unplugged. After a couple of months, when her father decided to purchase a television set for the house, my grandma was so happy she couldn't stop dancing. When the TV arrived she watched it very enthusiastically for a few weeks after which she lost interest. She realized that she lost interest in that television set because it would be with her forever and nobody could take it away from her. The beauty of life can be explained only in death she told me, in the fact that it has to end. So, when she was actually dying I wondered if she still felt the same. I wanted to ask her but couldn't because she wasn't conscious in her last days. I wish she had opened her eyes and said something before she finally left. Said her goodbyes and gratitude's, maybe something, just anything. But she didn't say a word. Farewells are an important part of life, they give you closure, and the circle completes itself then. However, if the circle is left incomplete, it leaves a lot of space for emptiness and despair."

"She had always lived her life well and had told everyone that she had completed all her duties and had done her best to make all her dreams come true and was therefore ready to leave the world. She always wanted Rihanna and me to visit her homeland once and I wondered if this was one of those wishes she had pushed too much for but couldn't accomplish. I thought about this a lot but like all other thoughts this one faded too, but never fully. A lot of mixed emotions finally made me book my tickets to India three months after her death; there was the guilt of not being able to give her much time in the last years of her life, there was the desire to fulfill her wish, there was the need to travel and explore and the eagerness to feel good about myself by doing something for someone else – it was almost a necessity to get rid of that constantly fading yet never disappearing thought in my head. Of course it was also perfect timing because my family was going on their annual vacation to Dubai, which I was never too fond of anyway and preferred travelling alone during that month. But the most important reason Kali, was to find those relationships my grandma always talked about, the kind that stay on forever in one's heart, and which according to her could be found in India with just a little luck."

"You really loved her, didn't you?"

"I don't know. Never thought about it."

"What's the need to think?"

"I don't know. I always need to give my feelings a thought before I can actually understand what they mean."

"You did love her."

"I guess. I wish I had told her that."

"You know, despite everything, I still love my father. He was very fond of my brother and me, but something happened to him after my brother died. I think he couldn't take the pain. He became very aggressive and impatient and slowly our financial position went from bad to worse. He could handle anything I guess, but the moment he realized he couldn't feed his own family he died a little. He wanted to kill my mother and me so that we don't die of hunger. He wanted to kill me out of love. I know. Everyone has a different way of showing love and I think I understand my father today. His ways were wrong and maybe even he was wrong but I don't hate him. But my mother was right too. She was always stronger than my father. I know she loved him; she just wanted to protect me. She still loves him and that's why she is ready to spend her life in this rotten Jail. She is seeking redemption. Not from anyone else but from herself. She wants to forgive herself for killing the man she loved." She said in a very low but confident tone.

"Wow Kali, I am so proud of you. I wish I could forgive too."

"Forgive whom?"

"Adi."

"Aditya; your childhood friend?"

"Yes."

"Why? What did he do?"

"When I think about it now, I just feel stupid."

"Doesn't matter. Tell me?"

"Maybe tomorrow? It's getting too late. I have to get up in the morning and do a lot of cleaning work."

"No, please."

"Kali, you are beautiful. Hope you receive all the happiness there is."

"That means you are not telling me anything?"

"Not today. Tomorrow maybe."

She kissed my neck and fell asleep two minutes after closing her eyes.

I wasn't sleepy though. I could go on talking to her for hours but I was a little tired and even bewildered. She was making me aware of those emotions I hadn't even thought about. I didn't know I felt a certain way about something until I talked to her about it. Maybe this is what was missing in my life all this while I thought to myself. Maybe this was my whole. Everyone has ups and downs, inflows and outflows, and that is the entire point of life and I thought I was managing everything very well until Kali came along and showed me that all I was doing was piling up my emotions. Happiness and unhappiness. All you need to do is live an emotion fully and it will let go of you on its own. If something sad happens, be pathetic, be completely broken for sometime, and be honest about it. With yourself as well as with others and very soon you'll realize you're over it. That it's gone and you'll feel fresh. When something very wonderful happens, feel elated, go out with your family and friends, laugh and smile, live that moment fully and then sober up, let go of it. Don't depend on that one event for your happiness. I felt liberated within those four walls. I felt at peace in the most turbulent phase of my life.

I couldn't get any sleep that night although I had a really long day ahead. To think of it, all my days over there had been really long and the nights desperately short. I could hardly meet Kali during the day, since she went to school most days and even if she didn't I was busy with whatever duty I was allotted in the particular week. We would meet over lunch sometimes but could hardly talk freely. However, everyday I met someone new, made a new bond, shared something with someone, heard new stories, witnessed and felt almost every emotion that has been named and some that haven't been given a name yet. This was a completely new world; a world of extremes, where there was hope in every eye and yet, all hearts were full of remorse. Where there was anger and love in equal measure, where although every inmate felt like they had fallen in the deepest pit, they managed to find happiness in small things; the smallest of things.

X

It was after twenty days that I finally went to see the *pathshala* or the school of the Jail. It was an average sized rectangular hall that had two blackboards with a carpet placed carefully in front of both. In between the two boards was a wooden table and chair, which was meant for the teacher I assumed. The white walls had chart papers stuck all over, one of them had alphabets written on it in both Hindi and English, one had numbers from one to fifty, one had tables up to five and the other from five to ten. There was also a sketch of the human body with colorful arrows indicating each body part. Women from my *barric* had been going to attend 'classes' regularly but I never felt the need to find out the stuff they learnt and who taught them. But I was slowly beginning to get attached to this place and I wanted to go deep inside, to see everything there was to it, and so I decided to go.

By talking to a few people I found out that they have a permanent government teacher, who visits them twice a week but is completely useless as she just sits, gossips and leaves after three hours. The main work was being done by this organization; the inmates weren't too sure about the name of the organization but named three people: Heena *didi*, Azma *didi* and Khushi *didi*, who took care of everything. They visited four days a week and taught the inmates Hindi, English and Mathematics. All the inmates seemed to be deeply fond of these women, who would not only train them in academics but also help them get in touch with their families by making phone calls on their behalf or even visiting their relatives. They would also arrange lawyers for them and tried getting them bailed. I was lucky enough to not only meet them but also help them do their noble work.

Around 11:00 am people had started entering the room with one register and a pen placed neatly in a transparent folder, which had been provided to them by this organization. There weren't too many people, around 25 I believe. The Jail had over 300 women so this number was relatively small. I just stood at the gate and observed everything. Two women dressed in salwar suits entered the room. The moment they entered everyone gave a very heart warming smile, *"Namaste didi ji, kaise ho aap?"* (Greetings, how are you?) Everyone said almost unanimously. The two ladies seemed to be really affectionate and dedicated. One by one the women went to them and got their registers checked. Some had written letters, some had solved math sums and some had spelt words starting with different alphabets. Everything was in

Hindi medium except Math. After the ladies had checked all the copies, they taught the inmates how to multiply and then gave them sums to solve. Then both of them stood near the door where I was standing and began to talk.

"After multiplication, we need to teach them division, but what will happen after that? We haven't taught them English in so long."

"Yes, How will we complete their English course on time if we don't find someone to teach them the subject!"

"Just a month left for this semester to get over. I hope Khushi comes back soon."

"Yes. Let's hope so."

I grasped that they needed someone to teach English to the students because whoever had been teaching them English couldn't do so for reasons unknown to me at that moment. I decided to intervene hoping I could do something productive with my time here.

"Hello? Do you need someone who can teach English? Maybe I could be of some help," I told them.

"Hello. I am sorry I didn't see you standing here. You are?" asked the taller among the two.

"Ayanna. I am sorry I don't know your name?" I stated.

"I am Heena and she is Azma. When did you come here? We've never seen you before."

She was a very humble woman. She was slender and tall but had very evident burn marks all over her face and hands. Although those marks were very prominent and covered almost her entire face, there was a strange charm on her face, the kind that comes naturally.

"I came here about twenty days back." I told her.

"What have you done?" She asked me.

It was always so hard to answer this question. I almost had tears in my eyes when I spoke about it to Kali for the first time and so I had decided not to talk about it again. But with this woman it seemed like an easy task.

"It is a long story. Do you have time?"

"They will take at least half an hour to solve all the sums," she said.

"I am from London and was here on a one month holiday, if I may say so. The first place I visited was Lucknow because that was my grandma's hometown except I don't know anybody there. I was staying in a guesthouse and had hired a car to roam around in the city. I usually drive around in London but didn't know that the traffic in India is crazy. I accidently hit a car. There was a married couple in the car and because of the thud the woman hurt her head, which started to bleed. It wasn't a very serious injury and although I had hurt my knee as well I got off the car to apologize. That was my biggest mistake I guess. The guy went mad and started yelling at me as if it was entirely my fault. I was still being decent and offered to take his wife to the hospital except he was adamant to call the police. The first thing the police asked me for was something my car-hiring agent didn't ask for; my driver's license. I had a British license and it was illegal to drive in India using that. Things were still not as bad, and I could have gotten away really easily even then except that guy seemed to be on drugs. He wanted to take me to the police station and get me arrested. I did whatever the police asked me to do so that I wouldn't make matters worse. I wanted to clear the matter by paying the fine but nobody was listening to me. At the police station I found out that that car's driver was some small government officer in Lucknow, who didn't seem to be in a very good mood and decided to take out all his life's frustration on me. He lodged an F.I.R, accusing me of not just driving rashly and without a license but also attempting to murder his wife. Then they just arrested me. I was so taken aback at that time that I couldn't understand anything that was going on. Everything happened so fast, just half an hour back I was going to take pictures in old Lucknow and within no time I had been charged of attempting to murder someone, a person I didn't even know. Even though it was a very minor case it was blown out of proportion because the car I hit belonged to some government officer. Bad luck was all around me then, my car-hiring agent refused to help me because he thought he'd get into trouble for not asking for my license. I couldn't get through to my father but that wouldn't have helped me anyway. The only way to get out of that nonsense was to get someone to sign a bail and pay the officials some money. I tried explaining my case to them but they seemed to be enjoying the presence of a foreigner in their Jail. My problems got worse when they decided to transfer my case to the London Jail because it was against the law to deal with a foreign national in an Indian Jail. According to them I had to be punished as per English laws and so I was sent to the Central Jail while all the formalities of my transfer were being completed. They promised me it wouldn't take a lot of time and that they didn't have any other option. I begged, pleaded, wept and yelled but nobody bothered. All this was mere entertainment for them. Insensitive bastards. The jailer here told me that these "formalities" often take months to complete and that I am not anyone's priority here."

"I am not surprised. Nobody cares. The innocent suffer more than the guilty and nobody cares. You know out of the 341 women prisoners here around 250 are innocent and are paying a price for being illiterate and trusting their relatives too much." She told me.

"What?" I realized later that I almost yelled that out.

"Their family members don't want them back because they think about the number of mouths they will have to shut and hence, nobody gets them bailed, and for that matter nobody even comes to visit them. Most of them are from very poor families and therefore don't have the money to get a lawyer. It often takes years before the government can provide them with a lawyer to fight their case. These women are so kind hearted and warm, you'll never think of them as criminals if you sit and talk to them. I guess it is just really their bad luck; maybe the stars aren't on their side. What does one do! It's really sad!" She seemed terribly upset with the state of affairs.

I was shocked and saying that would be an understatement. It took me a lot of time to grasp what she had said.

"Have you tried to contact your family?" She asked me.

"For the first seven days I kept begging the warden everyday to let me make a few calls. She told me the prisoners aren't allowed to make calls everyday but offered help by trying to contact my family herself. She says she can't get through. I don't know whether she is dialing the right code or not, or whether her phone allows international calls or not, but the fact remains that she can't get through." I explained.

"Why just for the first seven days? Won't your family be worried?"

"That's another story. They are on a month-long holiday and according to them I am travelling. They know when I travel I don't usually stay in touch with anyone. Everything seems to be working against me. But I know they'll get really concerned if I don't call them for one month straight. I really don't know what to do."

"We work for a non-governmental organization here and help the inmates get lawyers etc. We could help you get in touch with your family and get you out of this place as soon as possible."

"The jailer here had called me to his office two days back, he told me the file has been signed and that it shouldn't take long."

"You don't seem to be very keen about getting out of here. This "shouldn't take long" could mean years. These courts, judges, government officers take years to solve even the smallest cases."

"This will sound weird and funny and I feel stupid while saying it but I am beginning to like it here. If someone asks me to leave tomorrow, I will be upset. This is a really messed up place but I want to stay here for some more time. I don't know. Maybe a week or a month more. I miss home and my family and I know they'll be worried but I wish I could do things my way: tell my family I am in a deep dark pit and that I am liking it there and still get hold of a ladder anytime I want and just climb my way out of this pit, carrying everything I want with me. I wish things were in my hand. I wish I had a little more control over my own life." I got goose bumps when I said this out loud for the first time. I was talking like that to somebody I had met just half an hour back and was feeling good about it. Kali must have really done wonders.

"This place isn't meant for you or for anyone for that matter. People have been stuck here for decades because they have no way of getting out and they still hope everyday, every single day that today someone might call them and tell them they are free to leave. Some have become mentally deranged because of sheer loneliness; a couple of them even tried to commit suicide. I come here for a few hours, teach them, help them in whatever way I can and then get back to my world. I am deeply attached to this place and everyone in here but I don't belong here. Don't get carried away by emotions. Life doesn't give you chances all the time." Spoke the wise lady and I suddenly woke up from my dreams.

"I'll give you the number, you could try calling maybe?" I said half-heartedly.

"I'll try my best." She patted my back.

The inmates had finished their math sums and were waiting for their papers to be corrected. Azma collected all the copies and kept them on the wooden table. We started correcting the copies one by one.

"When we started teaching here, two years back, in August 2011, these people didn't even know how to hold a pen. We are very proud of them."

"You're doing such amazing work. These women are really fond of all of you it seems."

"We are really fond of them too." She stated.

While we were busy checking the copies a middle-aged woman walked up to us and said, "Heena *didi*, did you speak to Rammanohar?"

She looked and sounded worried.

"*Namaste,* Laxmi *ji*! I called on the number you had given me. Your sister in-law answered but cut the phone when I said you have sent a message for Rammanohar *ji*."

"*Bahut pareshan hoon mein didi. Kya karoon.*" (I am very worried, what should I do?) She said with teary eyes.

"What do I say Laxmi *ji*. Be patient, something might work out." Azma consoled her.

After she had left, I asked Heena *ji*, "What was this about?"

I seemed to have developed this habit of asking too many questions from Kali.

"She is here under 302, murder of her husband. One day she had a huge fight with her husband and he left the house. When he did not return for a couple of days, Laxmi's brother-in-law Rammanohar lodged an F.I.R against Laxmi, stating that she had murdered her husband and buried his body somewhere. Surprisingly the police found the body near their house within a few days and later arrested Laxmi. She has been here since the past five years and hasn't had even a single court hearing ever since. We can't do anything unless at least one of her family member decides to support her. She still thinks that one day her brother-in-law will realize his mistake and come to her rescue but we know that won't happen cause he is now enjoying whatever little wealth his brother had."

"That's horrible. Do such people actually exist?" I said in disbelief.

"Even worse Ayanna *ji*." She sighed.

XI

Later that day, I met Laxmi *ji* outside my *barric*. It was almost dinnertime and I asked her to come along with me to the *bhandara* or the eating-place.

"*Namaste*! I can't come with you, I'll eat after half an hour," she told me in a low tone.

"Why not?"

"I am fasting."

"*Roza*?"

It was the holy month of *Ramadan* and all the Muslim women in the Jail had been fasting. They would eat only after sunset.

"Yes."

"But your name suggests that you aren't a Muslim?" I was a little perplexed.

"How does that change anything?"

"Isn't *roza* just for Muslims?"

"It is for anyone who believes in God."

Every day, each and every day, someone or something would leave me speechless. I felt so silly about myself and about everything I had seen and learnt over so many years. We give up on God so easily, as if we are searching for reasons to blame him, to curse him, to not believe in him. Although I was never a religious person, I did believe in some invisible force, which was holding things together. However, I was skeptical about my own theory half the time. And there I was standing in front of someone who had faced betrayal, loss, suffering, torture but was fasting for a God she still believed in. Not *Allah*, not *Rama*, but a God she believed in. She still believed. All my life I had been looking for that something to believe in, to have full faith in, and in that moment I wondered what was my reason for faithlessness in the first place? We just want to create a hassle about everything; we yearn for happiness but never accept it when it comes to us. What do we keep looking for, searching for, when nothing has ever satisfied us and nothing ever will? Honestly, I was mad at the world outside the Jail then.

"Can I wait here with you for half an hour?"

"No no, you must be hungry, you please eat."

"I am not."

She was wearing a pale yellow cotton sari draped carelessly around her lower body with a simple white blouse. She had covered her hair with the end of the sari and unlike a lot of other inmates she wasn't wearing any make-up or accessories.

"Do you enjoy studying?"

"Not really, but it is important. I will have to support myself when I get out of here and I won't be able to do that unless I am able to read and write."

"You are right. I hope you get out of this place very soon."

I was very awkward with my conversations with the inmates. I never knew what to do or how to react. I had never come across such situations in my life.

"Let's start walking towards the *bhandara*. It's almost time."

"Sure." I said.

"What is your week's duty?" She asked me.

"I am in the *saaf-safai* (cleaning) department. I informed her. "You?"

"Vegetable loading." She said.

There were around four departments in the Jail for work allotment. *Bhandara*, where one was expected to cook for all the inmates and also serve them; *saaf-safai*, where one was responsible for the cleaning of the premises; vegetable loading, where the job was to unload raw vegetables from the truck and bring them to the kitchen, and lastly, assorting rice and grains, to make sure they were insect free. This work would keep all the inmates occupied and not give them too much free time to pick up fights with each other. It also made sure that the work in the Jail was being taken care of. There were wardens to supervise the work except I found most of them inefficient and unsympathetic.

We walked the rest of the distance in awkward silence and I finally spoke when we had been served food and began eating.

"Have they ever changed the menu over the years?"

She laughed and said, "They haven't changed it in the last 2 and a half years at least. We joke about how they must have cooked large quantities of food and stored it somewhere and that they keep serving us the same thing over and over again, because it never tastes different."

"Five years is a really long time. I wonder how you feel." I thought out loud.

"You wouldn't have to stay that long. They are stretching your case unnecessarily."

"People tell me it could be because I am a foreigner?"

"I am not and still I am dying in this hell and nobody is even willing to listen to me. You belong to a big family; they'll let you go. When you don't have money, then it doesn't matter whether you are innocent or guilty, man or wife, mother or the child. You are just poor and that is all they see."

"Where do you think the government is going wrong?" I asked inquisitively. I had been brought up with such gentle care that I couldn't even imagine a life like this. I hated myself for the times I had whined because I didn't get anything on time or because of just nothing at all.

"Heart."

"Huh?"

"They don't seem to have one."

I could feel the anger in her calm voice.

"Anyway, you be happy, you'll be fine when your family comes here."

Every word she said pierced through my heart. I had money so I should be happy; she didn't so she may be stuck there forever. That man driving the car was a government servant so my minor crime becomes a major crime and now because I am from a rich family my crime would again become a minor one. Is this the world we are living in? Have we truly come down to this? And the answer was a mournful, resounding 'yes'.

XII

That night Kali slept before the warden locked the *barric* and when I got back she was already fast asleep. I felt strange because Kali never slept without talking to me. I saw her mother sitting next to her, sewing a handkerchief.

Sewing was everyone's favorite pastime in the Jail; the inmates were provided with cloth and sewing material and would make beautiful saris, handkerchiefs and kurtas in their free time. And they usually had a lot of free time.

"*Namaste* Aarti *ji*! How come Kali slept so early today?" I asked hesitantly.

"*Namaste* Ayanna *ji!* She wasn't feeling well, had slight fever. She wanted to wait for you but I forced her to sleep."

I hadn't really spoken to Kali's mother ever, although we stayed in the same *barric*. By then I had interacted with a lot of women but it would become a little awkward with Kali's mother for some reason. Maybe because I knew and understood her too well even before getting to know her at all personally.

"She is a lovely child." I said while watching Kali sleep.

"I know. She is the reason I am still living. Come sit?"

"Someone like her would definitely make living worth it."

"I don't know where she gets all her wisdom from."

"From life, maybe."

"I know I am responsible for all this. I wish I could have given Kali a better life."

"You have given her a life, and by this I don't mean birth."

"I know. But things could have been different."

"Things could have been different for anyone and everyone. The fact remains that they aren't and you need to deal with that."

"It's really easy to say certain things."

"You need to be a little hopeful about things."

"Hopeful about what?"

"A future? For you and Kali?"

"And hope my way into hopelessness?"

"You could make your journey to hopelessness a little better at least."

"But then what's the point?"

"The point is that you are still living and you can't live like you're dead. What if they free you tomorrow? What will you do? You'll be worse than you are now."

"I am not getting freed tomorrow."

"You are not willing to understand."

"I can't understand hope."

"Hope is what you want Kali to be. When you dream about that 'better life,' you are hoping. Everyone is hoping secretly. No matter how hopeless the hope is."

"But I don't want to hope. I have nothing to look forward to."

"Why don't you start studying?"

"What will I get by learning A B C D?"

"Something to look forward to."

"Hmm."

"Promise me you'll come for class from tomorrow?" I used the English word "promise" thinking she'd know the meaning.

"*Promees* means *vaada*?"

"Yes," I smiled.

"I can't *promees* you this then."

"Why not?"

"*Vaade tode nahi jaate!* (One must not break promises!) What if I am unable to come one day because of illness or some reason? I'll have to break my *promees*. So I'll come everyday, but I can't *promees*."

"Now I know where Kali gets it from. Goodnight."

I smiled myself to sleep that night.

XIII

When I woke up the next morning Kali was still sleeping. I touched her forehead gently to check if her body was still warm. She didn't seem to have fever.

There were 18 women in my *barric* including myself, and all of us would wake up as soon as the warden would open the gates at five in the morning; the sound of the huge bolt unlocking was too loud to be ignored. There were five washrooms outside the *barric* and two toilets inside. Everyone would take turns to bathe but this wasn't a very peaceful procedure. A few ladies were very nagging and would fight over things like soap and toothpaste. Every inmate was entitled to a soap dish and a small toothpaste tube in a month and since that wasn't enough for many, women would often resort to stealing and fighting. After this morning scene, the inmates would get back to their respective daily jobs; the ones who didn't have any set duties would sit and sew. Some would sit and do their school work, some would be busy cleaning the place or preparing food. Others would gossip about the wardens, the Jailer and other inmates. Apparently, I was a major topic of discussion during those days. Apart from waiting for some news from their family members, these were the things they could do or rather had been doing for years.

I quickly finished cleaning the *barric* and the other allotted areas for the day because I had to meet Heena *ji* at eleven. I was really looking forward to teaching English to the inmates and kept thinking about how I'll start and what I'll say while sweeping the floor. That day my back ached a little less and the floor looked a little cleaner. I had been cribbing about a backache ever since I had been allotted this duty but it was funny how that day I didn't feel a thing. Was it because my back actually didn't hurt although I was doing the same amount of physical labor or because my mind was in a better state, thinking about better things and hence couldn't concentrate on the pain? The latter, I suppose.

I reached the *pathshala* exactly at 11 but there was no one there. After waiting for sometime I was about to go back when I thought I had no other work to do anyway. So I decided that waiting was the best way to kill time. Inmates finally started coming around quarter to twelve.

"Where is ma'am?" I asked Nazreen *ji.*

"They must be coming."

"I thought they came at eleven."

"Must have gotten late because of some work. I heard you would be teaching us English because Khushi *didi* can't come?"

"Wow. Everyone already knows! I am not even sure yet."

"I don't know! Naseem told me."

I chuckled and said, "Alright. Can you read English?"

"Me? I am illiterate."

"Can you read and write Hindi?"

"Yes."

"Then don't call yourself illiterate. You are demeaning your own language."

She was about to say something when Heena *ji* entered and asked everyone to sit down. She announced that I would teach English from today till I was let out. I thanked her and took charge of the class. On the first day I remember teaching them about vowels; all of them knew the alphabets and a few other basics. Since I didn't have a lot of time in hand I was glad I didn't have to start from the scratch. After one hour of teaching, I gave them a little fill in the blanks exercise.

While everyone was occupied with completing the classwork, a little kid, aged eight maybe, walked up to me and asked, "Namaste *didi*, you know English?"

"Hello young man, yes I do. What is your name?"

"Roshan. Can you tell me something?"

"Yes of course." I hadn't interacted with any of the other kids around. There were six-seven kids other than Kali but none of them stayed in my *barric*. That's why I never got a chance to talk to them.

"What do you call *gareeb* in English?"

Without reading too much into the question, I answered, "Poor."

"Am I poor then?" He asked innocently. I was a little taken aback and didn't know what to say. Again.

"Why? What made you think so?" was all I could come up with.

"My teacher wrote 'poor' in my math register." He said and left me looking at him, wondering, if I could do anything at all to get him out of this place.

I hugged him.

"That poor means poor work, love."

"That means I am not poor?"

"You are adorable."

He blushed.

That was my first day at class and I went on teaching everyday and learnt more than I taught.

XIV

"It was raining and the road outside our house was almost flooded with water. My father made paper boats and we floated them in that water. It was so much fun to watch those paper boats survive the stormy weather and reach the other end of the road. Some of them tore midway but that was expected so it didn't make me sad." Kali told me when I asked her about her happiest day.

"What made this day so special, *Noor*?"

"All of us were together and everything was fun, even the torn paper boats. Out of all the days I somehow remember this one clearly. I can almost hear the sound of our laughter even today."

"You're too wise for your age, you know. Don't worry, you'll have happier days, you have a long life ahead of you."

"I want to believe you."

"You must."

"You tell me about your happiest day now." She demanded.

Happiest. I never kept a record of my days, never maintained a scrapbook or a diary and that question triggered a wave of thoughts. One by one moments were flashing in front of my eyes: my convocation ceremony, the day I got a job as the editor of UK's best travel magazine, when I was awarded a gold medal for excellence in academics, when I went skydiving, when my mother bought me an iPod - there were so many happy days. But I couldn't think of that one day, which could be called the happiest.

"How did you decide on your happiest day? I don't know mine."

"It is the only day I want to live again and again."

"None then. I don't wish to relive any moment, I'd rather see another day, better or worse."

"I like you. I want to be like you."

"I like you too. And I wish I was more like you."

We both laughed.

After talking about her day at school and how she didn't feel too well in her English class, she asked me how my day had been. I told her about school and what I taught and how initially I had never even imagined teaching the very people who scared me at first. To which she said, "Why did they scare you?"

"Because I didn't know them. The unknown is always scary I guess."

'You like travelling, you should be loving the unknown."

"Not in that sense Kali. Before travelling I research and I have a good idea about all the places I'll be visiting. Here, it was all too sudden, I couldn't understand anything and there was nobody to help me. It was too dark and I felt lost and lonely. It reminds me of the time I went deep sea diving."

"Deep sea diving? What's diving?" She understood the English words "deep" and "sea" but couldn't understand the meaning of "diving."

"Jumping sort of, except you jump in the sea. But I think what I did was deep sea crawling, I crawled from the shore to the deep sea."

"Why would you do that? I've heard the sea is very *very* deep."

"For fun. I have always been slightly adventurous. But this wasn't particularly fun for me."

"Why?"

"I'll tell you a secret. I am a little scared of deep water."

"Why is that a secret? At least you know you are scared of it. There is a possibility that I'll never get to know."

"You always make me feel silly."

"So why did you decide to do deep sea diving when you were scared?"

"I didn't know what was coming my way. It's very safe; they provide you with safety equipment and train you for hours in shallow water before taking you to the deeper parts. I wanted to do it because I felt like trying something challenging and new."

"Then what happened"?

"We were three of us, including the trainer. My practice session, in which they teach you how to breathe underwater and tell you about the various signs used to communicate, went really well. I was very happy and told the trainer I was ready to walk to the deeper level. We had to hover close to the ocean floor till we were 15 meters under. Kali, how I felt then would describe exactly how I felt here. When we finally reached around ten meters deep, I decided to look on either side for my two companions but couldn't find anybody. It was so dark Kali. Not dark blue but pitch black. When I looked above, I felt like it would take me forever to get out of there. I felt breathless, suffocated and suddenly I forgot all the breathing exercises that I had learnt just a few minutes back. I wanted help and I could see nobody. I have never been that scared and it was all because it was too dark and deep and I didn't know how far I had come and how long it would take me to get back to the surface. To get back to my world, to see my parents standing and waiting for me at the shore, to go back to the place where I could breathe normally. I had lost all sense of time and place and I didn't know how to get it back. That was terrifying. I remember standing somewhere in the middle of the ocean, wanting to yell for help, when someone suddenly held my hand. It was my trainer. I looked at him and signaled him to take me to the surface, struggling to tell him that I wasn't okay. He asked me to hold on, held my hand tightly and kept moving forward. I was still tremendously scared but had faith in my trainer. We floated deeper into the sea while all my concentration was focused on not loosening the grip of our hands. He came in front of me and gestured me to look around. Kali, what I saw then was just beautiful. Vibrant schools of fish surrounded me. I could touch them; they were soft and delicate. It was incredible. The red and orange corals looked gorgeous and I could see fish hiding inside them. It was a completely different world Kali. Even the rocks and stones were so attractive. It was getting darker and I was going deeper but I could see things now, beautiful things. On moving a little further I saw a small cage. I was hesitant to go through it, but my trainer, whose hand I held firmly, asked me to give it a try. I believe those were the best few seconds of my life. Everything inside the cage was shining so brilliantly. It was flawlessly beautiful, as if someone had stuck diamonds all over it. When I wanted to touch a few things, my trainer signaled me not to, maybe because they were poisonous or dangerous and yet, so stunning. After floating for some more time, we removed our weights and within a few seconds reached the surface where I could breathe normally again. I was glad I made it to my world but what I left behind had completely changed the way I looked at it. I am still scared to go back you know, but that feeling changed me. Deeper, darker and so much more beautiful. I wish I could tell you in better words, but I am afraid I don't have any."

"You wouldn't want to go back?"

"Maybe not."

"I would want to if I were you."

"I think I am still a little scared to feel that helpless again."

"But somebody was there to hold your hand."

"You know that you are that person here, right?"

"Yes, I know." She held my hand then and it felt like I could see the beauty again. That was the first time in so many years that I felt like somebody knew me too well and also the first time that I was really afraid to lose somebody.

"Why can't things go the way we want them to?" I contemplated.

"What's the point of living then?"

"You're right. It could be because there is something better in store for us?"

"Not necessarily and not always. But that's how you should think, that's the only way one can be happy in any situation."

"That's absurd. We will be living in false hope then."

"No hope is false. There are so many possibilities in this world, there are miracles and there is magic, and haven't you asked me to believe in all of this?"

"Once in a while I need reminders about my own conceptions and theories. It is really hard to keep believing in one thing for a long time." I laughed.

"I am here to remind you."

"I wish you are always there to remind me." I looked at her and smiled.

"There are miracles and there is magic, *Ummi*." And both of us giggled.

XV

Everyone deserves a fair chance but I was living in place where hardly anybody got one. So many pending cases, so many inmates still without a lawyer, so many people confessing that they were guilty just because they knew that the court procedure could take longer than the period of sentence for that crime. So many people just waiting, longing, seeking, praying, hoping, yearning and wishing. Things with no definite end. You could go on doing these things forever; things that are endless. But you still do them because that's the only option left. At least inside the four walls of a Jail, where every second of your existence is painful. Either it doesn't let you forget something you haven't done or constantly reminds you of something you've done. Either you come out of the prison to a world that doesn't belong to you anymore, or you die waiting. It was so hard to maintain your sanity in such a state and maybe that's why there were so many cases of mentally deranged women in the Jail. I was an exception of course. Amid all the craving and struggling, I was surprisingly at peace.

At times I felt like a rich spoilt brat, who had been temporarily deprived of her comforts and was enjoying the new twist in her life. I would tell myself then, 'you shouldn't be feeling good, you should be howling and screaming.' Honestly, a strange sense of security surrounded me; I was almost sure I would be out of that place soon because no matter how harsh, the truth remained that the entire system could be bent with money. But sometimes I would be trapped between all the *what ifs*: what if my family never finds out where I am, what if I never see Kali's face again, what if? There were reasons to stay and I found that disturbing. There were so many negative-positive emotions and feelings. Despite all of that I was at peace. I didn't wait for news from my parents or the Jailer, I just waited for the next day, the next night, the next thing to learn, the next emotion to feel, the next time I'll be left speechless, the next thing I'll teach, the next time I'll give one of the inmates a reason to smile, the next time I'll discover something new about myself and so on.

I was lying on my mattress, staring blindly at the night-sky, when suddenly Kali's voice broke my trail of thought, "The moon looks so big tonight, no *Ummi*?"

I suddenly snapped out of my thoughts and took a while to affirm her statement, "Indeed Kali, I didn't even notice it until now."

"What were you thinking about?"

"Everything that's going on."

"Are you sad?"

"No, and I was wondering why."

"Why aren't you allowing yourself to be happy?"

"It's just strange Kali. I am not entirely happy but I am at peace with it."

"So just let it be. Why do you have to keep thinking about it till you start feeling sad?"

"That's how it should be, right? I should be frustrated right now."

"Who gets to decide that?"

"That would happen under normal circumstances."

"Once my mother told me she was feeling very happy in the Jail, I asked her why and she told me that it just felt like a good day. I was a little confused and asked her to explain why she felt that way because in the Jail almost all days are identical. She told me that she had allowed herself to be happy and decided to forgive herself for one day. I found the idea so absurd. If she could do it for one day and be happy, why couldn't she just let it go and be happy always? We think we should feel a certain way in a particular situation and force ourselves to feel like that even if we truly don't. The norm says that I should be sad right now, so I will be sad even though I am not. We are always so scared to let go of these emotions and I can never understand what makes us so scared. Why can't you just feel happy if you are happy and feel sad if you're sad? If you don't miss home, why is that a big deal for you *Ummi*? Allow yourself to be happy even in this situation." She spoke so confidently that for a few minutes I forgot that she was just a 12 year old. But by then I had realized that she wasn't just another child and hence didn't feel the need to tell her again that she was too wise for her age.

"Maybe you are right. Maybe it's all about giving yourself the permission to let go." Even I wasn't sure what made us so scared.

"Why does the moon look so big today?" She would often shift from one topic to another while my mind would still be stuck on the previous one.

"Huh? Oh, It must be full moon night."

"As in?"

"The moon has phases. As you know some nights it hides itself completely, some nights it shows itself partially and on a few nights, like tonight, it shines and glows with full power, making the world look so much brighter. The funny part is we are still seeing just about half the moon."

"Why does that happen?"

"You want the scientific explanation?"

"Anything that would explain why this happens."

"It's because the earth is moving around the sun and the moon is moving around the earth. So the distance between the sun and the moon determines the latter's size and shape."

"What role does the sun play?"

"The moon doesn't have any light of its own, it reflects the light of the sun."

"That's disappointing." She was frowning.

I laughed, "Is it, why?"

"I always loved the moon for shining so brightly at night and making everything look so beautiful but it is actually the sun shining and not the moon."

"Knowing too much can be a little disappointing sometimes."

"Um, I don't think so. I'll just thank the sun for making the moon look so beautiful from now on."

"You sweet kid. I love you."

"You are beautiful, *Ummi*." She said.

"Maybe I am just reflecting your beauty, *Noor*."

"Can you sing a lullaby for me tonight?"

"Is anything disturbing you?" She hadn't asked me to sing her to sleep ever.

"The fact that you'll leave me soon and I'll never see you again."

" You want to put your head on my lap?"

"No, but please put your hand on my head?"

And then I sang for her softly. I remember making up a lullaby then, I can't recall the exact words now but it should sound something like this in English:

"Little Kali must close her eyes,
Little Kali must rest now,
Tonight a little more love I will send,
Something's go on forever, something's never end.
Little Kali it's time to dream,
Little Kali loves the moonlight now,
Tonight a little more hope I'll send,
Something's go on forever, something's never end."

She slept in no time but I couldn't get any sleep. I was still caught up in our conversation about the moon and the sun. Maybe the moon shines because it has a companion. A companion for eternity. Maybe it is this security, which makes it burn so bright. Maybe.

XVI

Anjali *ji* introduced me to Era that day after class. She told me, "Ayanna *ji*, I don't care too much about myself anymore, I have spent a very good amount of my life here. But she is young and innocent, and I am very worried about her. She is from Bangladesh and can't even talk in Hindi properly."

It was breathtakingly amazing how they still cared about others. How they didn't want anyone else to suffer their fate.

"Hello Era, I am Ayanna. What's your story?"

She burst into tears as soon as I said that, as if she had been holding up for really long and had suddenly seen a familiar face or heard a familiar voice and was in her comfort zone again.

"Hey, don't cry. That doesn't help. What happened?"

She took a couple of minutes to compose herself before she finally spoke, "I didn't do anything, I promise I didn't, those assholes! They said they will give me a good job in India, but they, they..." she started sobbing again.

"They what?" I asked out of concern.

"Call girl. They asked her to become a prostitute after they got her to India." Anjali *ji* spoke on Era's behalf. She almost whispered those words as if to make sure that nobody except for me heard them.

I had read that this happened everywhere, in so many countries, with so many girls, but I had never imagined that one such girl would come crying to me someday asking for some help. I tried consoling her, "Era, listen to me, don't cry please. You don't have anytime to waste." I said a little sternly so that she would take it seriously.

"They took me to a red-light area and kept telling me that there is nothing wrong with sleeping around for money. And that it was just a business. I was howling and they didn't listen to me. The next day the police came and arrested me. I don't know why and I don't know anything. I want to go back home. I want to go back. Please take me home."

"It is a business Era. People do it willingly and there is nothing wrong with it."

"I don't care ma'am. They told me they'd give me a well paying job as a hotel receptionist. They are assholes."

"That's pathetic. You need to calm down. Have you spoken to your family?"

"What do I tell them? I got caught in a red-light area?" I felt really stupid for asking that question.

"It isn't a severe offence. You'll be out in no time."

"Three months they said. But why? Why should I spend three months in imprisonment when I haven't done anything wrong?"

"Get a lawyer? Fight for your rights?"

"The men who got me to India arranged a lawyer for me yesterday."

"What?"

"They told the police they are my brothers. I don't want their help; they want me to get out of here so that I can help them get business."

"So you refused the help?"

"They weren't helping me, they were helping themselves. I don't want to go back to that hell."

"What will you do now?"

"I don't know. I just don't want to go back with them."

"There is this organization that helps inmates get lawyers. You could get their help."

"Yes, Anjali was telling me about it. All this is just not right.. Not right.. So unfair.. What did I do to deserve this"? She was still crying.

"Era, you need to compose yourself. Be patient, it will all be okay." I was saying what I thought I should be saying, not what I actually wanted to say. I wanted to tell her that she was no one to decide what's fair and what's unfair, that we need to face things in life and that crying and howling is not the answer to anything. Instead, I consoled her, comforted her and gave her a shoulder to cry on and that seemed to be working pretty well.

"I want to get out of this place soon." She just wouldn't stop.

"You aren't the only one, sweetheart. You'll be fine."

I asked Anjali *ji* to take her to her *barric* and decided to discuss her case with Heena *ji*.

Heena *ji* would usually stick around for sometime once class got over because after she had played the role of a teacher, she would take up the role of a friend and counselor. I saw her standing outside the *pathshala* talking to a bunch of women. I went up to her and asked, "Heena *ji*, could you please give me five minutes?"

"Yes of course." She promised the other women that their work would be done and asked them to come for class the next day.

"What happened?" She asked me. I wouldn't have disturbed her meeting under normal circumstances, so my intervention gave her the hint that something was wrong.

"It's about Era. She came here yesterday. Did you hear?"

"Yes. It's really sad. Don't worry, it is a cycle. The initial days always involve a lot of howling and crying."

"But can't we do anything about it?"

"Of course! We'll try! Like we always do."

"Will it work?"

"Our job is to give it our best shot. There have been some battles that we have fought successfully and in some we've been defeated at the very beginning. There are so many people sitting above us. We don't even have a fraction of the power they yield. If they decide to take a lunch break when someone is dying in front of them, we have to comply. That is how it is."

"I know. But there is some good left, right? Your organization, for instance, reflects that good."

"The good is very determined to make a change, but is pretty powerless to say the least." She was smirking.

"She shouldn't be here. Those bastards should be in jail."

"Neither should you, or more than half the people here. But you are, and so are the rest of them."

"You can't be looking at things this way. At least not you."

"I am just telling you the truth and simultaneously I am also trying to change the truth."

"What's going wrong?"

"What's not going wrong?" She paused for my response but when she realized I didn't have anything to say she added, "I have been doing this job for over ten years now and even today, these cases stir me up emotionally and I feel things can change. And that is a very strong reason for me to still be here."

"That's what I needed to hear. Why can't the government create more courts, appoint more judges and lawyers, increase the working hours, give them more money so that they don't have to rely on the rich to pay them. Why is justice taking so much time?"

"You can't give all of them a heart too, right? Everyone's thinking about themselves and their families, and there is nothing wrong about it but this selfish love is making them heartless."

"Um, let me know if you need any help?"

"Don't worry. I'll do my best, like I always do."

"You are doing great work, you know that right? You are like that light one sees at the end of a dark long tunnel."

She laughed.

"You are mad!"

"Can I ask you something if it is not too personal?" I asked hesitantly.

"I don't think I have anything to hide. What is it?"

"Why do you have burn marks all over your face and upper body?" I had been meaning to ask her this question ever since I met her but didn't know whether it would be appropriate or not.

"Um, my husband poured acid on me while I was sleeping." There it was: another reality, another truth, another life and another story.

I didn't know how to respond so I just stood there in front of her in complete awe.

"What happened, Ayanna *ji*?" *What happened*, she asked me.

I remember her tone so well even today; it was like when a magician performs his best trick and leaves the audience spellbound and speechless and later asks them very carelessly, "What happened? Did I just do something?"

"Nothing. No really, nothing." In that moment I could have either told her that she had inspired me in a way nothing or nobody ever had, or not tell her anything at all. I chose the latter then.

"Where is your husband now? I didn't even know you were married."

"He committed suicide by drinking the same acid with which he scarred me for life."

She sounded angry, maybe a little, the type of anger that doesn't have any meaning or significance in your life anymore but yet she sounded angry.

"Why would your husband do that to you?" My eyes felt warm; I think I cried a bit then.

"He was insecure. I was the only one earning for the family and he was too egoistic to accept that he was useless. Um, also, he thought I was too beautiful to be trusted."

"That's disgusting."

"It sure is. It's been seven years now. Although the physical scars have stopped hurting, the mental ones still strike the wrong chords sometimes."

"You couldn't get justice so now you make sure everyone else does?"

"If you want to think about it that way. Though I wouldn't like to give too much importance to that incident, because that would mean my husband played a prominent role in making me who I am today and that wouldn't be true."

"You are an inspiration. I don't know what to say but I just hope with all my heart that you get whatever you wish for."

She laughed, "Don't look at me differently after listening to my story please."

"I can't help it. I am looking at you differently, with a lot more respect and love."

"I think I'll leave. I am getting late." We suddenly realized we had been standing and talking in the sun for more than half an hour.

"Thank you."

"For what?"

"You'd never know and I'll never be able to explain."

"Okay, I'll leave then. And we are trying to get through your family."

"Bye Heena *ji*."

And she left leaving a smile on my face.

XVII

Kali had been regular with her English work and hence was learning very swiftly. She was reading and speaking fairly well in no time. She also wrote most of the words I dictated with just minor spelling errors. I remember one day when I was teaching her tenses. Past. Present. Future. She was quick to grasp the concept and after one hour of teaching she was giving me examples of her own.

"You had to tell me about Adi." She used this sentence as an example.

"Past tense. Yes."

"No, future."

"Why?"

"You had to but you didn't and now you will."

She wasn't very fluent but decent enough for me to understand what she was trying to say. She would generally take the help of Hindi words to complete her sentences. A lot of hard work was required and both of us were willing to do our best. I was only afraid that we were running short of time. I wanted to fulfill my promise. I had learnt the value of a promise from Kali's mother and I just knew I couldn't leave things mid-way.

"Tell me?" She insisted.

"Kali, we have the whole night left to talk about Adi. Can we study right now?"

I would never talk to her about leaving or having less time together. At the very least I would avoid initiating the topic because that would make both of us feel low.

"But we have done our bit for today. Please *Ummi*." I always thought I was stubborn till I met Kali.

"You will never give up, will you?"

"You asked me never to."

"Uh-huh! It's so pointless arguing with you."

"Tell me *Ummi*."

Over the past one-year so many people had tried to talk to me about him. But I had told them I have stopped caring and so should they. This could be because I knew talking about him would do no one any good, especially not me.

"Aditya was my neighbor. Rihanna, Adi and I would play together all the time. If I ever think about my childhood I always recall having the fondest memories with Adi. He was always around in the last 24 years and so I had never really imagined a life where he wasn't present. He wasn't a best friend or a brother, not even a lover; he was just there, always, without any tags, without any expectations or demands. You know the kind of people who don't make any promises but end up being the ones to keep so many unsaid promises? The ones who don't make it to your secret diary but when you think about them you realize that they have somehow always been a part of all the significant things in your life. You know how we take the most important people for granted because we have a false sense of security that they'll be a part of our lives no matter what? I don't know Kali. I don't know what went wrong or rather who went wrong. He proposed to me last year. It was the day I had my graduation ceremony. Aditya had come to attend the ceremony along with all my family members. He asked me if he could take me out for dinner and I said yes because trust me Kali, I had no idea he was planning to propose. We had never had intimate talks about love, or even friendship. At least not about our love and friendship. He knew about my boyfriends, my break ups, and everything else but never in our conversations did he tell me he liked me. How was I supposed to know what was coming my way Kali? I didn't know how to react when he told me he loved me. I tried laughing it off at first but then realized he was serious. He told me he had always been secretly in love with me but never had the courage to say it out loud. You know more than anything else, more than any other feeling or emotion, I felt cheated. Everything just suddenly flashed in front of my eyes: him always being around, always trying to make me happier than I was, always planning those little surprises for me, being there for everything that was important to me. I was trying hard to think about the times when I needed Adi and he hadn't been around but there were none. And I felt cheated because he was there in anticipation of his love. It was the reason for his presence, and if this love hadn't been there, he wouldn't have been there either. When he proposed to me, I knew this was the end because the moment I reject his love, he'd drift apart."

"What did you tell him then?" Kali asked because I didn't say anything for a long time.

"I told him I didn't feel the same for him. I hadn't thought about him as the person I would want to spend the rest of my life with, in fact I hadn't thought about him at all. Kali, it was so hard to explain it to him. I told him everything that would soften the blow but it was certain that it wouldn't work. He didn't take it well Kali. He didn't say a word. He just left. Later he asked his employer to transfer him to their offices in New York City. He left Kali, without any goodbyes or farewell gifts. Without any sweet sounding words or a tight bye-bye hug. And I was expected to just accept it, just accept the fact that he loved me and because I didn't love him back, he wouldn't be a part of my life anymore. I was so mad at him then and I suppose I still am. I was just so disappointed in him for feeling that way and for just kicking me out of his life when I didn't feel the same way. I tried getting in touch with him but he just sent me a message saying, 'I need sometime, give me time and I'll be okay.' So I gave him time. I had so many things to look forward to then and although Adi was almost always there at the back of my mind, I decided to be okay without him. It was hard but I don't think there was any other way out. On certain days I would just sit down and wonder, what if he called and told me he has moved on and that he wants to be friends with me again. What would I say then? Could things ever be the same way again? Deep inside I knew they couldn't, no matter what."

"That's a very selfish way to look at it." She pointed out.

"Selfish?" I was confused.

"He loves you *Ummi*. You can't be mad at him for that."

"I am mad at him for ruining things between us because he couldn't deal with his feelings."

"You look at this as ruining things for you? He must be miserable. You lost a friend, he lost a lover and a friend."

"That's not fair Kali. He doesn't get to take all the decisions and leave me to just accept them."

"And nobody gets to decide what's fair and what's not. Didn't you tell me that?"

"But he didn't even give me a chance to heal him, to make things better."

"He didn't need you to heal him. It must have been so hard for him to leave his home, his family, his friends, his love and go live in a different place."

"I know Kali, and I understand it, but where did I go wrong here?"

"Nowhere. My mother once told me that we all plan things, we choose a path for ourselves and walk on it, till we come to a point when we realize that our path isn't a straight one. It is intertwined and interwoven, different paths cut across our path, and one fine day when we look back at the path we had planned to tread on, we realize that that path was never truly ours. Our lives are interconnected and sometimes we suffer because of others, and get hurt even when we don't deserve the hurt. This is the price we pay for our interconnecting paths because when we look back we'd prefer interventions and crossings and cuts to a lonely dull road." She would talk about these things with such innocence that I couldn't help falling for her everyday.

"I am amazed Kali. When did your mother tell you this?"

"When my brother died."

"My little love, you make the world a better place. Did you believe your mother? Did it make things better for you?"

"No, not until now."

"How come?"

"I can't be mad at all the lamps in the world because my brother died of an electric shock, I can't be mad at my dad for beating me up because he missed my brother, I can't be mad at anything or anyone because there is no point to this anger. Everyone is suffering. Some suffer more, some less and that doesn't change anything. If you were disappointed, Adi was heartbroken. I am not saying your suffering was less but he doesn't deserve your anger."

For one full year I had been struggling with my anger and love for Adi and in a few minutes she made me realize that I was wrong. I remember being so overwhelmed at that time. I was so full of emotions, I could physically feel them welling up my throat.

"I don't know what to say Kali, I feel silly."

"Why? You are the best."

"Just for you. Otherwise, I am very ordinary."

"I don't know about the otherwise, but for me you're the best and that is what matters."

"I love you?"

"Yes you do."

XVIII

I remember that day I had learnt that happiness could be found in small things, in fact, in anything. For the inmates happiness meant a little salt in the vegetables served to them, a new face in the Jail, solving a math sum, wearing new clothes that someone donated. It was the morning of my last day in the Jail, the fortieth day. I was teaching a very happy and efficient bunch of students that day, happy because they had been given new registers by the organization and efficient because they were happy.

I remember I was explaining Rani *ji* the difference between singular and plural words when my warden entered the class.

"Ayanna, you've been called by the Jailer."

"What happened?"

"Someone has come to meet you."

Those words. Whenever I think about those words I feel a shiver run down my body. For forty days I had been wondering about my reaction when someone finally comes to see me and I could never come up with a single emotion that I would feel then. But when someone finally said it, when someone finally came, I just ran. Without thinking about anything or anyone, forgetting about the promises, the love, the lessons, the discomforts, I just ran towards the main gate with joy.

When I think about that moment now, I just want it to come back again, just that three minute run from the classroom to the main gate because in those few minutes I felt nothing but happiness. I wasn't thinking about the consequences, I wasn't thinking about what would I have to forgo to get back to my previous life, I wasn't thinking about anything at all, not even happiness for that matter. I was just feeling without thinking.

When I reached the jailer's office, I saw them there, after so long. My family: *maa*, dad and Rihanna, sitting in front of the jailer's desk with tears in their eyes. Tears, which signified the pain, they had gone through. And then I cried, exactly like I had cried forty days back, when I had first come to the Jail. I went down on my knees and howled. What was the reason? Everyone thought I was venting out all the emotions I had felt in the last forty days but now I know what it was. The wait was over, the uncertainties had disappeared, and I knew in that moment that I had to leave because it was finally time and that I ought to be leaving and nobody can stop me, not even me. I couldn't understand myself back then though.

One by one, they came and hugged me hard and kept asking me if I was doing okay. They told me that the worst was over and that everything will be fine once I step out of that place. I didn't know what to say or do, I just cried.

"*Beta*, we've taken care of everything. That government officer has taken his case back. You are free now, don't cry baby, you're going home today." Dad told me.

You are free now. What is freedom? What does it mean? Isn't inner freedom more important than freedom from confinement? I had changed but I didn't realize it back then.

"Don't cry, baby, please don't cry. It's all over now, you are going back. Heena called us day before and told us everything. It's all okay now, please don't cry like that." *Maa* kept saying these words over and over again.

It's all over now. It was finally over and I shouldn't be crying because it was. Did I want it to get over? Why was I crying?

"Go get your things, we're flying back to London tonight." Said Rihanna.

Go get your things. There wasn't a single thing, apart from Kali's card that I wanted to carry with me. There were people, moments, memories, emotions, lessons and conversations that I would have liked to carry. Why didn't you give me that option back then, Rihanna? Weren't these things more important than the things you wanted me to carry?

I finally spoke.

"I can't leave right now. I have to wait for a while." I realized Kali would be in school and nothing inside me would ever forgive me if I left without saying a goodbye to her. I had to say something to make her feel good and maybe make a promise to come back. I had to capture that one last image of her in my heart before I left her, before her *Ummi* left her without fulfilling any of her promises. I had to ask her if she wanted to come along, I had to convince her that she should. I had to tell her she'll be fine, tell her one more time that she had made me happier than anyone else, that she will always remain the light of my life. I had to peck her forehead, I had to look into her eyes again, I had to take her along with me, I just had to.

"Why? We'll miss the flight *beta.* Everyone at home has missed you enough, we can't let you stay in this hell for even a second more." Said *maa.*

Why. What do I tell them? How do I explain anything to them at all? Do I tell them about Kali? But they'll never understand. Do I tell them about school? But they'll tell me I have better things to do. Do I tell them everything I learnt? But I won't be able to do that. Do I tell them how a part of me never wanted to leave that place? They'll think I have gone mad. So, this is what I said, "*Maa*, please let me stay here for a couple of hours more, I have certain promises to keep."

"Don't be stupid Ayanna. What promises? Just get your stuff and come with us." She answered as I had expected her to.

I started walking towards my *barric* to collect the card Kali had made for me. That was the only thing that I owned actually. I hadn't been given the time to take my things with me, and whatever I wore or ate or used had been provided to me by the Jail or the inmates. I reached my *barric* and saw those faces I had been seeing everyday since the past forty days, who had been there for me when I didn't have my family. Every face was associated with a story that had taught me something meaningful. I didn't have the courage or the right words to say goodbye to anyone of them, so I decided to leave without informing. I knew even back then that farewells were important and necessary but then they were also hard and I didn't have the strength.

When I picked up that card and saw it again, I got a feeling of leaving something unfulfilled. It was the worst emotion I had ever felt, except I didn't know back then that that is how I will have to feel for a very long time. I tore a piece of paper from Kali's register and wrote a little note for her.

"My Noor, the day is finally here. The day both of us were always afraid to talk about because it caused us too much pain. My parents have come to take me home and I don't have the words to make them understand how desperately I want to see your face once. I wonder how words always came so easily when I spoke to you. I am leaving alone Kali cause I know you wouldn't leave your mother even if I asked you to come along with me. I know I haven't kept my promises and I can't begin to tell you how much that hurts but I know you understand me, better than anyone ever did. Forgive me for leaving without completing the circle because I know I won't be able to forgive myself.

I'll miss you every second of every day and I'll hope I see you again, because you made me believe in hope. You'll keep lighting up my world for years to come Kali, and I hope I do the same for you. Shine on because you're my constant, my north star, who'll guide me always, even in absence. You'll grow up in no time and childhood memories might get blurred but please don't forget me cause I never will. I don't need to say anything else, I have a feeling you know everything already.

I have written my contact number and address at the back of this sheet. Send me word and I'll come running back to you.

Love,
Ummi."

I wished in that moment to do something else for her, give her a gift or leave some money behind for her future. So many thoughts crossed my mind but I didn't leave behind anything apart from that letter for I feared that would seem like I am paying her a price for leaving so unceremoniously and she wouldn't like that. I left the letter in her register and went to meet Aarti *ji.*

"Namaste!"

"Ayanna *ji,* come sit. I am having a little problem with this sentence."

"Aarti *ji,* I am leaving. My parents convinced the officer to take his case back, they have come to take me home." I had controlled my tears by then but when I said that to her my eyes became watery again as if I was finally telling someone who might understand a fraction of what I felt.

"All of a sudden? I am very happy for you but wait for Kali at least? She'll be so hurt."

"I know but I can't. I have to reach the airport on time. Aarti *ji,* please listen to me. Here is my address and contact number. If you ever need anything, remember that someone is just waiting for an opportunity to help Kali. I am leaving my constant with you, and one day, even if that's after 12 years, you feel that I can give Kali a better life, please let me know. I'll always feel the same for her."

"Take her with you Ayanna *ji.* She'll ruin her life in this Jail."

"I told her but she wouldn't listen, she doesn't want to leave you."

"I think I knew that already."

"Please take care of yourself and be hopeful for yourself and for Kali."

"Try visiting us sometime again?"

"I won't make any more promises because it hurts when we are unable to fulfill them."

"I'll miss you Ayanna *ji*, there were so many things left to do."

"I'll miss you too. Please don't let Kali hate me."

"She can't and you know it."

I hugged her and left for the other world, a better world as they called it.

PART 2

Present: 2014

"Our lives are interconnected and sometimes we suffer because of others, and get hurt even when we don't deserve the hurt. This is the price we pay for our interconnecting paths because when we look back we'd prefer interventions and crossings and cuts to a lonely dull road." "Kali was right Ayanna." I was sipping my morning coffee and updating my blog when Aditya entered my room and said that. I immediately got up from my chair and began searching for the book I had been writing about the forty days I had spent in the Jail, about my relationship with Kali, about the bonds I had made in confinement, about the forty days that just weren't enough and yet just about enough to change the way I looked at life completely. I called it *The Conversations I had Then*. I didn't want to publish it; neither did I want anyone to read it. It was meant for me, a record of those forty days, to read in

those moments when I needed inspiration, when I wanted to feel real, when I needed to know it actually happened. I never wanted to forget even a single conversation. At other times I wanted to erase those forty days completely, not because they were horrifying but because they changed me, and change for me has always been frightening. They left me with a constant feeling of being called out to, of something being left undone, of promises that needed fulfillment and of unspoken words that needed to be heard.

"I am sorry I read it. I needed to know what was going on in your mind." He said after five minutes of watching me go through every shelf and drawer in my room looking for the book he held in his hand.

I took the book from him, turned over to the first page just to ensure everything was alright and kept it on my shelf again, "Why are you here Adi? I don't need you here."

"I figured that out last night when you didn't even bother looking at me." I was seeing his face after five years today. The last time I saw him was at that restaurant, when he professed his love for me. I was slightly mad at him for reading the book but a part of me was content. Someone else knowing exactly how you feel makes things better. I would never have been able to explain things to him myself anyway.

"Then why are you still here?" I asked him very politely. Anger didn't come to me easily anymore. Kali was a good teacher; she taught me all the lessons very thoroughly.

"Because I need you to know that I am here for you."

"Suddenly after five years?" I had forgiven Adi a long time ago. I had stepped out of the Jail holding no grudges against anyone. I had learned to be completely honest about my emotions but I missed Kali because although I spoke to people about everything, I felt like people didn't listen. I missed getting inspired, I missed being heard, and I missed listening to what truly mattered. Although I had left Jail as a completely different person, the people and the life outside were exactly the same, the way I had left them when I had decided to go to India. They hadn't met Kali nor had they been moved the way I had been. I constantly craved for what was real and nobody seemed to be offering me that.

I had tried to get in touch with Adi many times in the last four years after moving back to London, but he never responded.

"I am sorry Ayanna. I know I have hurt you deeply and that I haven't been a friend to you but I need you to know that I have loved you, every single day. If I have stayed away from you, its because I wanted to protect you." He explained and I think I understood. As much as I wanted to be mad at him, I couldn't manage it. I didn't feel the need for anger since I knew that it wouldn't change anything for the better.

After leaving the Jail, I often tried to think like Kali. Initially it didn't come to me naturally, but over the past four years I have become more and more like her. I just hope she is still the same, wherever she is. However, sometimes I do struggle, like this moment today, because thinking like Kali wasn't easy.

"I want to be mad at you Adi. I just feel like you've missed out on everything. I feel so far away from you now."

"Be mad then. I think I deserve the anger."

"What's the point?"

"Maybe you'll feel better after being completely mad at me."

"Hmm, you shouldn't have read that."

"I know but there was no other way in which I could find out why you suddenly left everything and came to India."

"So now you know?"

"And I think I understand too."

"You do?" It was strange to finally talk to someone who was at least willing to understand why I felt a certain way.

"Yeah, I guess I know how it feels."

"Didn't *maa* send you here to take me back?"

"She did, but I came here to see why you don't want to come back."

"It's not like I don't want to come back Adi, I just cannot be at peace with myself there. I need to be here, doing what I am doing. This gives me the peace I need. I am not waiting for Kali to come back every second, I just need to know she is fine. I need to say something's to her and that's it. I don't think I am here just for her, but yes, I am here because of her. I am here because I am a changed person. I don't feel the need to do what I was doing all my life anymore. As much as I want to go back, I can't, because I've changed, without even realizing it. I know I can't be at peace anywhere but here."

I suddenly realized, Aditya stood exactly where he was standing when I first saw him this morning. I pulled a chair for him and tapped it, asking him to sit down while I sat on my bed, right in front of him. After two minutes of silence, he spoke, "You know why am I here?"

I looked at him waiting for him to answer his own question.

"Because I realized I am at peace when I am with you. I understand myself better when you're around."

"Still?"

"Remember it's not about letting go, it's about holding on?"

I smiled. He was echoing Kali's wisdom in his voice and I liked that.

"I am happy you know Kali now. I hope you meet her one day."

"I hope so too. I think I have become really fond of her just in one night."

"She is magical."

"I am sure. Miss her?"

It was such an obvious question but still nobody had asked it to me this directly ever. My family kept hoping I'd forget about those forty days and pretend they never happened. They asked me not to tell people about my experiences in India because that might ruin my image in society. I listened to them not because I understood their reason but because I knew that if my own family didn't understand me, nobody else would.

"I can't explain Adi. I just need to know where she is; I need to know she is alright." I always tried to avoid this thought as much as I could.

"I am sure she is." He reassured.

"When did you come here Adi? What about your work?"

"Came here last evening. When I came to your room yesterday, you seemed really lost and I knew you wouldn't tell me anything. So I picked up the book lying on your desk. I hoped it would give me an idea of what you're going through. I am sorry, I know I shouldn't have."

"It's fine. I am not mad at you. What did *Maa* say?" I know my family had been really worried about me. I hadn't put across my situation in front of them in the best way. They had suddenly seen me change after those forty days and although the change was mostly positive for me, I think they just thought I hadn't taken the entire episode too well and needed time to go back to my normal life. When that didn't happen, they got pretty worried.

"She told me about how you had left for India six months back and were not willing to come back. I am assuming you haven't spoken too openly about this to her because she didn't seem to have any idea about what was going on in your mind."

"I wanted to tell her so many times. I tried, but every time she would think of me as some little lunatic who had completely lost her mind because of some traumatic event. I wouldn't even expect her to understand Adi, I don't think I can expect anybody to understand me. But I have never been so sure of anything all my life."

"I am really glad you know now. It's the best place to be. So, how is work coming along?" He asked me while making tea in the little kettle placed on the side table of my hotel room.

"Exactly what I want to do." I said with certainty.

"So I am assuming you are working with the same NGO that you mentioned in the book? They teach people in the Jail?"

"Yes. I am glad you read that book, makes things so much easier." I said it with a smile but I think there was a fine line between sarcasm and humor in my tone.

"But they do way more than teaching, they help innocent women inmates get lawyers and also send messages to their families. They put their heart and soul into their jobs for hardly any money."

I had been working with their organization since the past six months and I couldn't see myself doing anything else. I would work all day, trying to create awareness in people about the situation of these women and getting them as much help as I could. I presented their cases in front of lawyers and had been quite successful in bringing some inmates in front of judges. I would often visit the families of these women and try to instill some sense into them. Mostly they were nice and asked me to leave politely, but sometimes I had to face the brunt of their anger. I visited the 'Mahila Niketan Jail' twice a week and continued teaching the inmates English and Mathematics. The women were doing well and we were planning to start computer lessons for them once we got the permission from the superintendent. Other than working with the Jail inmates, I also helped the organization deal with other cases of violence against women. I did everything ranging from counseling to fieldwork, to spreading awareness on social networking sites. Doing all this work made me feel close to Kali, although I had no idea where she was or what she was doing. I'd go to Jail every time with the hope that she would come to visit her mother and I'd be able to meet her but that never happened. I kept busy; I knew I was doing the right work, and I was at peace here. But amid everything, amid all the voices and the silences, I just wanted to hear that beautiful voice call me *Ummi* one more time.

"I am really proud of you." He offered me a cup of tea while holding his cup in the other hand.

"Oh, you made it for me too? I just had coffee." I took the cup from his hand and kept it aside.

"The weather is really nice today. Do you want to go out for a walk?"

"You don't want to have your tea first?"

"No, I don't think I want to."

Adi, I contemplated, had always been like this. He gave too much to others, be it love, attention, care or time. I never realized the importance of this back then but now that I wanted to give exactly those things to others, I understood how much it took to not put oneself before others.

"You haven't changed at all." I told him while putting on my overcoat.

"I have, but couldn't bring myself to change for you. Let's go?"

II

It was a cold November evening, and as we walked along the narrow footpaths of Lucknow, I guess I found my old friend again.

"So, tell me, what happened after you left India for London?" I knew he'd want to know about my journey and although I was secretly praying he'd ask me this question, I did not know whether I had an answer that would explain everything.

"It's a long story, I don't know where to begin."

"Begin from the end of your book." He said and I couldn't help smiling.

"I might sound like a lunatic to you in the next couple of hours but try not to think of me as one. I have never felt so real about anything in my life and although I know the life I lived before going to prison was way easier, this life makes me feel closer to myself and to others. I'll never be able to go back to how I lived earlier. You know how I was always all about exploring, visiting new places, meeting new people, trying different things? I always wanted to see the better side of me, I always wanted to go one level up, and if that didn't happen, I wouldn't take it too well. If anything or any person were not in sync with the way I wanted things to be, I'd just let go. I'd cut them loose. I was always too scared of getting too attached because of this reason. I wanted to soar high and I didn't want anybody to hold me back with the strings of attachments. There was always this sense of emptiness though, and that made me worry. Those forty days in the Jail, when I didn't have any of the other things I just mentioned, I didn't feel empty. When everything was going wrong, this one thing was going completely right and it made me realize that's all I needed."

"I wish I could tell you how I felt back then Adi, when I was leaving that Jail without Kali, without even seeing her face. To be honest, I didn't realize the importance of that one goodbye until I reached London. I was back to my normal life: coffee with cream, comfortable bed, dream job, best friends, loving family, but all I craved for was that feeling of not longing to go back. I tried really hard to get rid of that constant sound of someone trying to call me, or the tune of the lullaby I once sang, humming in my head almost all the time. I tried not to think about Kali every time I looked at the moon but couldn't quite manage it. It wasn't because I needed Kali, it was because I needed to know if she is alright, whether she is mad at me, if she misses me or if she has already forgotten about me, if she read that letter I left for her or whether it flew away before she could even read it. I needed to know how she reacted when Aarti *ji* told her I had left. The fact that I couldn't find out these things created so many uncertainties that I was slowly yearning to go back to India just to see if everything was fine. I didn't want Kali to forget me Adi. I couldn't explain my situation to anyone. I looked normal to people but my mind just wasn't in the right place. My parents began to worry when I tried my level best to contact this NGO in India and even get in touch with the Central Jail. Even if they understood me, they really wanted me to move on. I completely understand that, but I couldn't help it Adi. I had learned how to hold on and was doing exactly that. I felt so silly for not taking anyone's numbers, but it all happened so quickly, I couldn't even help it. I wished every moment I had said my goodbyes, given everyone a hug, said sorry for not being able to teach them English because I knew they really wanted to learn. They are such great learners; if you met them you'd know. I lost interest in many things I had enjoyed earlier and that wasn't because I wasn't full of life anymore but it was because I saw life in better and bigger things. The meaning of life had changed for me. Life meant bonds for me, it meant doing things for others, it meant feeling complete even though you have nothing. Life for me was that core I ran away from earlier."

"I did manage to contact the NGO and that gave me a sense of comfort. Heena *ji* told me everything was well and although everyone misses me a lot, they are all doing okay otherwise. When I asked her about Kali, she told me she didn't see her often. But I called and questioned her about Kali so many times that she finally met her for my sake. She asked Kali how she felt about me leaving so unceremoniously. Apparently, Kali told Heena *ji* that she missed me, but also wished me all the happiness in the world. She asked Heena *ji* to tell me to not worry about her; that I should now live my life like I was in that little cage under water, which I described to her in one of our talks. She didn't want me to be scared Adi, she wanted me to see the beauty even when I was aware there is darkness outside. She was talking about my diving experience and how I should not think about the loneliness and the darkness underwater but concentrate on that little cage and the beauty it held, and it is only then that I'd be willing to gather the courage to go under the sea again. Do you see what she did here Adi? She said exactly what I needed to hear, gave me that motivation again. She was asking me to not be scared of the unknown. Hearing what Kali had to say and that she was doing fine made things so much better for me. I started living life again. I called Heena *ji* often until one day I just couldn't get through. I was cut loose again but this time I told myself that everything in that Jail was fine. I told myself they didn't need me and that I didn't have to think so much about it. Kali, I assumed, would have probably found her hope in someone else or would have found a companion in some other inmate. This thought made me so insecure but I knew it was good for her, so I let things be. I decided not to try to remind everyone of me all the time. I knew that Heena *ji* has my number; she'd call if she needed me for anything. I wanted to be at peace again and although not even a single day went by when I didn't think about Kali and the other inmates, I resumed my normal life. It was after two years that my company offered me a job in Los Angeles. I decided to take it up immediately because I thought a change in place would be good. It was only later that I realized I was not about travel and change anymore. The one-year in Los Angeles went really well. I don't remember having a single dull moment. I met the best people, had amazing conversations with them, and earned a lot of money by doing what I thought I wanted to do. There was a constant sense of friction though, something that was just not going right. I was elated, proud and full of life but I wasn't whole. I was just about almost whole and I didn't even know what to change. The moon still reminded me of Kali, and I missed her voice so much but I didn't want to think about those forty days. I didn't want to take any big steps; I didn't want to feel my core because I knew it would change things for me. I was still scared Adi. I was still scared of going underwater. All this while I was thinking I have overcome my fear, but I was wrong. I was still so afraid of taking big steps."

I almost broke down while saying that and I could feel the slight shake in my voice. I think Adi noticed it too and that's why he ruffled my hair and said, "All of us are scared Ayanna. Don't make it so big in your head. We all have our fears and anxieties and it's perfectly okay to be scared and miserable sometimes. Most of us live our lives hiding away from our own fears and never wanting to face them. You, at least, had the guts to face them and for that matter, even overcome them."

"I took almost four years to overcome my fears and although it doesn't seem like it, it was a long time." I paused for a little while, looked at Adi, and gathered the courage to speak the next few words, "Things could have been different."

"Different how?"

I had missed Adi in the last five years. His genuine concern for me always made it easier for me to talk to him and reveal my emotions.

"You're a great friend. You know that, right?" I hadn't welcomed him in the best way and although I was extremely happy to see him again, I didn't know how to react. There were so many emotions playing inside me that I didn't know which one to single out. It was comforting to have an old friend around in a place where I was making new bonds everyday.

"I am sorry it took me so much time to be the great friend you are talking about. I was so entangled in my own feelings, and so desperate to get out of that trap that I really couldn't think of anyone else. It was only later that I figured out certain things about myself."

"Like what?" I completely understood Adi's feelings. This was the one thing I had learnt back in Jail. I knew he was talking about his love for me and although I still didn't love him the way he did, I realized that the bond we shared was stronger than any of our efforts to let go of it.

"I couldn't get out of that trap. I ran away from everything only to realize I was running in circles. I never thought I'd create such a mess. I disappointed so many people, especially you. I didn't know a feeling could grow to be so big. I didn't know that a rejection from one person could pierce me so deep and when it did, I didn't know how to deal with it. You were always the closest to me and I left you without even saying goodbye. I was so guilty but I didn't know how to face you again. I am glad you didn't see me in the last five years. I have been able to rebuild what you are seeing today only after a lot of hard work." His words were so full of hurt and yet they sounded so warm.

"You didn't deserve to go through all of this. I am sorry."

"You don't have to be. It made me a better person and I am glad you were always honest about your feelings. It was my fault that I didn't have the strength to face the truth."

"But you really didn't deserve it Adi."

"Neither did you. I know how you feel about Kali, Ayanna, and I also know that you'll have to deal with your feelings alone. I am glad you're doing something great while you're at it."

I chuckled, "Great wouldn't be the best word to use here mister."

"It's best when you don't know you're doing something great." We both laughed and in that moment I knew I was in the right place, sharing my feelings with the right person.

III

"So, how could things be different now?" He hadn't forgotten about my story while narrating his.

"Kali might have been with me right now." It's funny how these *what ifs* always manage to blur the line between hopefulness and hopelessness.

"How did you realize that things could have been different had you taken these big steps earlier?"

"*Hm*, my work period of one year in LA was over and I had moved back to London. After a few months of being in London, I found an envelope lying in my *maa's* cupboard and it was addressed to me. It was from India."

I paused.

"Did Kali write to you?"

I knew Adi was attached to my story by now, he had read the book and he was probably the only person who knew what Kali meant to me. I could feel that in his voice.

"Yes Adi, she wrote to me. She sent a letter to me all the way from India, and you know when I saw it? A year after she posted it."

It had been about a year since that incident took place and I could still feel the anger in my voice.

"You know the sinking feeling you get when you are sitting on a roller coaster and you feel like they haven't strapped you securely? That sudden feeling of panic, helplessness, excitement and fear? That's how I felt when I saw Kali's name on that envelope. I didn't know what that letter contained or how she sent it, all I knew was that that letter had been lying in the cupboard since the past one year, and I knew that one year could have changed a lot of things for her. I zoned out completely in that moment as if that moment was all I had. I knew it; I knew that that was it. No matter what that letter contains, it's going to change me again, and this time I wouldn't be scared to face the changes."

"Why didn't anybody ever tell you about the letter?" He asked.

"I was so furious Adi. They thought that I was finally getting over those forty days on account of moving to LA and although they knew that letter would mean the world to me, they didn't want to push me back into the memories of those 'brutal' days. What could I have done? The damage had been done and now the price had to be paid. I was so mad but what could I have told them? How could I have been mad at them for thinking about my well-being? But how could they not give me that letter Adi, when they knew I always longed to hear from those people? How could they just assume I was over those forty days? How could they have not thought about Kali? Maybe she was in trouble, maybe she needed my help? How could they?" I think I was still venting out that anger because I didn't take it out completely back then.

"They thought it was good for you Ayanna. They obviously didn't know it would make things worse. I can imagine them being so scared for you." His words helped me add some practicality to my sudden emotional outburst.

"You are right, but the thought of how different things could have been almost kills me."

"Things could have been different for anyone and everyone. The fact remains that they aren't. Remember saying this to someone a few years back?"

I smiled, "How do you remember these details?"

"Let's just say I read the book too carefully."

"I am glad you're here."

"I'll be gone soon though."

"When do you plan to go back?"

"I am flying back tomorrow."

"Why this early?"

"I just came to see you."

"Um."

"You're doing fine."

"How do you know that?"

"You are sure of what you want, and this is exactly what you want."

"This?"

"Yes, this life here, this work you're doing, this wait that you know will end some day, this feeling of being almost whole, of almost reaching your destination."

"When will I finally get there?"

"Wait for the right time, and be happy while you're at it."

"Didn't you tell me that it's been too long?"

"I didn't know your story back then. Sometimes, long just isn't long enough."

"I never thought you'd understand me so well."

"You never gave me the chance to."

"Maybe it all comes down to that. Taking risks, giving chances."

"Maybe, but no chance that you love me?" He laughed in a subtle way.

"Um." I didn't know what to tell him, I never looked at him as a lover and I couldn't change that.

"I didn't mean to put you in an awkward situation, I was just fooling around."

"I know you weren't Adi. I wish I could help you."

"You are, you always have."

"Thank you for coming."

"Thank you for sharing this part of you with me."

"It wasn't that hard."

"I am glad."

Both of us suddenly realized that we'd been walking since a very long time and decided to go back to the guesthouse. I had rented a room in a guesthouse in Lucknow. It was perfect for my needs as it was close to my office. I didn't want to buy a house here because I didn't want my parents to feel that I was going to stay here all my life. Things with my family were going well now, although I understood their point of view completely, I needed them to understand mine too. Over the months, they had realized that this is the life I've chosen for myself and that I will not give in easily. They had come to terms with my situation and in fact, both of them followed all my articles and posts on networking sites and newspapers. This might not have been the life they had dreamt for their daughter and it wasn't the life I had envisioned for myself either. But this was it, and it gave me the peace no dream job ever did.

IV

We ordered food because both of us were too tired to cook.

While having dinner Adi resumed the conversation we were having an hour ago, "What did Kali write in that letter? Can I read it?"

"It's best if you read it in Kali's words. I'll just give it to you." I went to my cupboard and took out the two things

Kali had given me. The letter that she sent to London and the card she made for me when I was incarcerated.

"This is the card she made for me. Isn't it beautiful?" I was so excited to show these things to someone.

"Wow, that is indeed very beautiful." He took the card from my hand and turned it around to see the little red heart on the backside.

"It feels rather nice to see this at last. That book, you should publish it." He held the card really delicately. Maybe because he knew it was my most prized possession.

"No, it's for keeps. It's my memory."

I never wanted to publish that book, firstly because it was too personal and secondly because it was incomplete and I didn't even know whether I'd ever know enough to complete it or not.

"It's your choice. Can I read the letter?"

"Hmm, sure. It's in Hindi though, you might want me to translate it."

"Please."

I had not made anyone read that letter before. I did mention some of the contents to a few people because I needed to explain to them the *whys* and the *hows* and the *why nots*.

"Beloved Ummi,

I am sorry I couldn't reply to your letter sooner. I didn't have the money to post it and hence I thought, what's the point of writing one. I have missed you a lot, not only me, everyone here: Anjali aunty, Laxmi aunty, Radha aunty, they all miss you too much. I always thought you were only my Ummi, but it seems like everyone looked at you as their Ummi too. I am 14 now, and my hair has grown longer; you might not be able to recognize me when you see me. I really wanted to write to you in English but then there would have been no point in sending you this letter to your far away place if you couldn't understand half of it (although I feel you might have been able to understand).

I am sorry Ummi, but I don't remember your face clearly. I wish you had left a photo of you with me. I try recalling but I am not able to see a very clear image ever. That makes me sad sometimes, but Ammi told me that that happens when you don't see a person for a long time. Now I wish I had seen you more than the moon in those forty days you were here. The moon still looks the same, but I don't feel the same way about it anymore. I think I started loving it in the first place because of you. I saw its beauty only because of the light you reflected. I know I am saying too many things at the same time but I am writing whatever is coming to my mind. I have so many things to tell you. I wonder how will you react when you read this.

I am sorry I wasn't around when you left, I regret not being there even today. That day when I came back from school, Ammi told me you had left. I promise I didn't cry but I suddenly felt like I couldn't stay in this place anymore. I felt like a part of me had left this Jail already. I didn't feel the end though and that's why I have a feeling it hasn't ended yet. I know I'll meet you, I know this letter will reach you and I know you'll come save me. When I read your letter, I wanted to write to you immediately. I even spoke to Heena didi about sending it to you, but she said it would be too costly. I wanted to tell you to not feel bad about leaving without a goodbye, because I don't even look at it as a goodbye. We didn't say goodbye because it wasn't one. I needed to tell you that I was sure I'd meet you again. I wouldn't have left with you that day even if you had asked me to and even if I was desperate to go along with you because Ammi would be so alone in this place without me. She just has me. If I look at it like this, I am glad I wasn't around when you were leaving; it made things so much easier for both of us.

Am I still your constant? Your North Star? I wish I am because you're still my Ummi, my umeed. You were the closest person to me after my brother you know. I felt the same way when he was around, I didn't feel the need to be around anyone else, or meet anyone else. I was so complete. I don't know why I never mentioned this to you before. I think it was because I always knew I had a little more time with you. We should not take time for granted no Ummi? I think I have grown up a little but nobody seems to be pointing it out to me here, maybe because nobody has the time to see me grow. Nothing has changed here since you left: the Jail looks the same, everybody still gets up at the same time, eats at the same time, sleeps at the same time. We still get the same food too. Some people have left the Jail though, and some new women have come here. Your life must have changed a lot, right? Do you remember all of us clearly? What new places did you visit? Did you go for deep sea diving again? Were you scared? You shouldn't be. I don't see the point of being scared. If I ever find out I am scared of something, I'll do it more, so that I can get rid of my feeling of fear. It must be such a bad feeling? Is it? Don't live all your life feeling something bad.

I had to tell you something; I am leaving the Jail tomorrow. The jailer says I am old enough to live without my mother now and that they can't keep me in because I am 14. There is a rule that children above the age of 13 cannot stay with their mother or father in prison. I don't know what to do. I wish I had a little control over things. Why do they take all the decisions for me? Ammi is really upset but says it's good for me in a way. How is it good Ummi? She tells me I shouldn't be punished for what she has done anymore and that I should go out and do better things. Do better things for whom Ummi? What's the point of freedom when it can't be shared with people? I don't know anybody outside these four walls except you, and you seem to be so far away. They are sending me to a government 'children's home.' I didn't even know what it meant until I asked my teacher at school, who told me that children who don't have parents are sent there. I don't understand this. I am hoping Ummi, I am hoping for a miracle to happen. What if they don't let me see Ammi? I think this is what fear feels like. Does it? It is such a bad place to be in. You were right about the unknown being scary. Not knowing what is going to happen next is frightening but I still want to see what's coming my way. Isn't that how it always is? We never know what's going to happen next but somehow we are always sure. Right? We make plans and are almost always positive that they will work out. Why? Why are we so sure Ummi? I want you to answer my questions. Whom should I ask if not you? I sometimes try thinking what you would have told me in a certain situation. I fail most of the times but sometimes it works. You are a wonderful companion even in absence. Still, I wish you were here to sing me to sleep.

When the jailer told my mother that I would have to leave the Jail in one month, she didn't know what to do. I wonder how she felt Ummi. I know she has made it through all these years only because I was around to love her but then I know she always struggled between wanting me to be with her and wanting me to do something good with my life. She finally took the decision when this situation came her way. She tells me I have a long life to live and that I should figure out a way to live a good one. How? You think I'll be able to? I don't even know what the world outside this Jail looks like. What if they don't send me to a school? I am not even worried about myself. I know I'll be okay. What will happen to my mother? Am I asking too many questions? I always asked too many questions, right?

I don't think you know how much everyone here misses you. They all really wanted to learn from you. You were a good teacher and you know why? Because you never looked at yourself as one. They were all sad that you left without meeting them. They think they weren't important for you but I know why you left without a goodbye. You didn't want to add another memory right? I know you loved them and I am sure you still do. I have faith in you and I know you'll be doing well, wherever you are.

Do you think this letter will ever reach you? I asked my teacher how to send you a letter. I earned some money in my school fair by selling handmade wristbands. I know you'll ask me to save the money for a bad day but I don't even know what is going to happen when I leave this Jail. From the moment Heena didi told me you need money to send a letter, I promised myself that this was the first thing I would do whenever I got a little money. If this letter reaches you, I'll be the happiest person.

The first thing I am going to do tomorrow, after leaving this Jail, is post this letter to you. I know you'll get it. Do you know how I know? One night, long time back, I saw a shooting star and as soon as I closed my eyes to ask for a wish, I thought of you. I didn't make a wish back then, but I know I am secretly working towards that wish I never actually made and I thank that star even today for making me realize what I wished for. I don't know where I'll be when you receive this letter but remember that wherever I am, my biggest wish would be to see your face again someday, even if it is only for a little while. Just so that I can be reminded of the way you look, so that I can ask you questions and know I'll get my answers eventually, so that I can look at the moon in the same way again, so that you can put your hand on my head just for little while, maybe just one more time?

I love you.

I am sending you word Ummi.

Yours,
Noor."

I didn't want Adi to realize that I had noticed the tears in his eyes. So I quickly folded the letter without making any eye contact with him, kept it neatly in the envelope and placed it carefully in my cupboard.

"What would she have done Ayanna? You didn't find her in the children's home?" I had thought about this so many times in my head that someone else asking me this question suddenly gave me a blood rush. The feeling you get when an emotion hits you physically. When your entire body realizes your heart feels something.

"I wish Adi. I really really wish I knew." That is when I broke down.

It was beautiful how even after all these years Kali could move me like this. How she could still make me feel so real.

Adi and I spent the rest of the evening talking about old times. We spoke a little about how our lives used to be, and a little about how things have changed, and somewhere while discussing what has changed; I think we realized what hasn't.

V

"What happened when you came back to India?" He finally spoke after a couple of minutes of silence.

I was driving him down to the airport. Our conversation was left incomplete last night because of my sudden breakdown. Adi didn't bring up that topic for the rest of the evening because he knew I needed time to calm down and think about something else.

"I had called Heena *ji* before coming and she had promised me that she'll try to find out the address of that children's home. We figured out it is called 'Baal Kendra.' When I reached Lucknow, the first thing I did was visit that place. I wish I could explain how I felt while that old lady was going through the list of the children admitted to the center. She went through every name, scrolling down her records with a pencil placed delicately between the tip of her thumb and index finger, repeating Kali's name under her breath. As if she would stop any second and say, "There! She is outside playing with the other children." But no, that didn't happen. She looked at me and said, *"Kali naam ka toh koi baccha nahi hai yaha."* (There is no child named Kali here). That is when I began to panic. I asked her to go through all her records from the past year and show me photos of the children if possible. Adi, I went through the list again and again and looked at all the photos several times but I just couldn't find Kali's name or photograph. You know how sometimes your world stands still? When you know that this moment might change everything. I felt so cold and weak, as if someone had drained out all the energy from my body. I was so powerless in that moment. If there was actually no record of Kali there, where could she be? And then a series of questions crossed my mind, questions that seemed to have way too many answers, and none of the answers were comforting. I didn't know what to do. I felt so heavy and weak at the same time, as if someone was adding more weight to my body every second and my fragile body just couldn't take it." I recalled.

It had been almost seven months since this incident took place. I had treaded a long way in this period but I know that I changed my path because of that one moment.

"Then? Did you ever find out anything that would lead you to Kali?" He questioned.

"After doing a lot of research, meeting the police many times and going through all the records, I found out that Kali was in fact admitted to that center but after a month or so of staying there, she suddenly disappeared and nobody knows where she went. The police are searching for her but you know how these things work. I did whatever I could possibly do to find her but couldn't."

"I am sure she is well Ayanna. Don't worry. I know you will meet her again."

"How are you so sure?"

"Why? Aren't you?'

"What makes you think I am sure I'll meet her?"

"I have never seen you like this before. It's as if I am with a different Ayanna right now."

"What do you mean?" I think I knew what he meant, but I just wanted him to say it.

"It's this spirit of yours. I can feel it when I am around you. You are so raw and yet so strong. And I know you are like this just because you are hopeful, because you know that your wish will come true."

"Wow, thanks." I didn't know what to say.

"Don't let anything bring you down. I will handle your family back home. You're doing the right thing."

"That makes things so much better for me. Thank you for coming."

"I am glad I came. Can't believe it's almost time to head back."

"You need to come back again soon."

"I will. I will come back to meet Kali."

I looked at him and smiled, "You know the right thing to say."

"I meant it."

"You be good. Alright?" I knew that although he'd never show it, he was still struggling with his feelings.

"Waiting is hard. Um, You'd know. But I am sure we both will be fine." Both of us laughed about it as if it didn't hurt us anymore.

We had reached the airport and it was time to say the final goodbyes. We hugged each other tight and then he left, but what he left behind was enough to replenish hope within me. My old friend had given me a new lease of life.

PART 3

Few months later

I resumed my work after that goodbye with a sense of freshness. People, who spent their days doing things for others, surrounded me all the time. And this constantly made me feel wonderful. I saw women walk into that office with tears and misery in their eyes and walk out with a hopeful smile after talking to the members. I saw each and every member work hard to make whatever little difference they could, because they knew it mattered. They knew that little steps would add up to a giant leap. We did everything we could, from staging street protests to fighting cases. Everyone there had suffered and now they were making sure nobody else did. Everyone had a secret place within themselves for their sorrow but nobody ever let that bring them down. It was almost as if they had replaced it with hope. Everyone was looking at ways to give something to the world and in that they found joy. It was a small family, not connected by blood but by something deeper, something intangible. Something that could be felt in every spoken word and experienced in every unspoken emotion. However, sometimes there was no hope: some cases were very hopeless and in those instances the emptiness of sorrow was replaced by the acceptance of it.

Days and months passed by and I never felt low. I was always occupied with work, the kind of work that gave me a sense of peace and purpose. A lot of things happened in my first year of working with the organization. We were being recognized, which is always a good thing for an NGO. This meant that people were supporting us, and so was the media. We had worked on many cases and had managed to give many inmates a new life outside the Jail. Some of them joined the organization and helped others while helping themselves. We also started a new project, wherein we would recruit girls from slum areas around Lucknow on the basis of a series of workshops and train them to use computers and cameras. These workshops were very basic and hence encouraged a lot of girls and women, who would otherwise be hesitant, to participate. We thought that teaching them how to use the computer would unravel the world in front of them, and the camera would give them an individual perspective and voice. Along with computer and camera learning workshops, we also had a monthly '*Nazariya* training' (perspective training), in which we would try to give the women a better, positive yet practical perspective about life and the society. During the training sessions we would try to break stereotypical views about men and women that were prevalent in the society, so that the girls could become powerful and strong-willed individuals rather than the fragile weaklings society had condemned them to be. This was done by making them watch movies and documentaries -- we would often shoot these documentaries ourselves - or through talks and storytelling. The amount of respect and love we received from these women was unimaginable. They would believe whatever we'd say and hence we had to be very careful while talking to them or while conducting these workshops. It was almost as if they had surrendered themselves to us in the form of clay and our task was to re-mold them in the right shape, in the given amount of time. Since I conducted quite a few of the photography workshops, I came very close to a few of these girls. They would sit with me for hours and just hear me talk, as if I was reciting the most stimulating story when often I'd be speaking about the most banal matters. It made me feel beautiful beyond expression. It's the most wonderful feeling in the world to know that your words have the power to change someone's life. I knew my words had that power, though with that came immense responsibility, which I was always aware of while speaking. I knew I had to pick my words carefully and therefore always had my guard on while communicating with them. I told them about the earth and its history, about India and its years of struggle and glory alike, about the continents and the wonders, about the places I had been to and the ones I wanted to see. They wanted to know every minor detail about my life, from what I ate to how many siblings I had, and I'd tell them everything because I knew they loved and respected me. They would question me sometimes, and as much as I waited for those questions, they always made me very nervous. Even today, after a year of interacting with different people and doing the same work, I feel that nervousness whenever anybody asks me a question in the workshop or even in the Jail. I was never confident enough and I think that is what Kali meant when she said that I never looked at myself as a teacher. It was true, I still learned more than I taught, and received more than I gave.

In one of the photography workshops, Rubeena, an 18-year-old girl asked me, "Why does everyone emphasize on perspective so much?"

"What do you mean, my dear?" Rubeena was always the quiet one. Amid all those reserved, shy girls who had joined our training, Rubeena was probably the only one who had remained unchanged. I never asked her to speak or open up because I understood that everyone takes their own time to make others read the pages from their story. She always looked at me with curious eyes though; eyes that often made me miss the grey in Kali's eyes. She spoke that day. After all these months of talking about perspective, she asked me why so much importance to perspective? I couldn't grasp what she was trying to say.

"What I want to say is, um, why are we talking about perspective all the time? How does it matter?" She sounded a bit mad at everything and that made me worry.

"Who do you think I am Rubeena?" I asked her.

"A teacher." She said without giving it a thought.

"No! I am not." I was trying to make her understand something, hoping I was heading in the right direction.

"Then who are you?"

"I am a student"

"That doesn't make sense."

"It does to me."

"But it's not true." She wasn't pleased with the situation I had put her in.

"I see myself as a student and you see me as teacher. We both have a different perspective about the same thing."

"But how does my perspective about you matter? It is what I feel and that wouldn't change anything"

"It is what you feel and that is what matters, right?"

"I don't understand."

"It matters the most Rubeena. If you stop looking at me as the teacher, you wouldn't value what I say and that would change our relationship completely."

"It doesn't matter in bigger things."

"What do you mean by bigger things?"

"Life, loss, poverty."

"Who told you that you are poor?"

"I know. I can see. I can see my house, my clothes, my life and I can tell that others are better off compared to me."

"That doesn't make you poor, does it?"

"I know you have money. You can say something like this so easily."

"I have money but I don't give it too much value."

"You have money and that's why you don't give it any value."

"This is your perspective and this is exactly why it's important. You compared yourself to others and thought that you were poor, right?"

She nodded.

"And you think I am rich?"

"What if I told you that you had something I really want but can't have?"

"That can't be true."

"I want to be your age. I want to be your age and be as wise as you are and see how you perceive the world."

"That's not possible"

"That makes you richer then. You have something that I want but can't have."

She smiled a little but didn't seem completely convinced so I went on to add, "I could look at everyone in a million different ways, but the one way I choose to look at them not only determines how they perceive me but also how I perceive myself. The world outside might look infinite and endless but it's not. The world inside us is much greater and richer because that world decides how we choose to look at the world outside us, whether as a mere dark black hole in the middle of the universe or as a land full of spectacular wonders and unimaginable colors. You might not have the money to buy expensive cars and clothes, but you do have a house to live in and a loving family, many don't even have that. Knowing where you stand when compared to others is a great thing, but it is your perspective that either makes you count the good in your life or whine about the bad."

"I like taking photos. It makes me feel I can capture my perspective."

"That's all you need to do. You only need to know what to include or exclude from your frame and then you'll just keep taking wonderful photos all your life."

"That sounds easy."

"It is actually as easy as that once you get the hang of it."

She laughed and I mentally patted my back thinking I'd done a nice job.

II

In the last one year every day had been a new challenge, where I had to make someone understand something I wasn't sure of myself, where I was asked questions I struggled to find answers to myself, where I realized that a lot of people leaned on me and I had to be strong enough to carry them. I saw miracles happen to others almost everyday, and I saw a lot of suffering too, but at the end of the day the feeling of belonging to that place compensated for all the minor obstacles I faced everyday. I felt like my love was needed here, and that made me feel so loved.

Apart from the work at office, the work in Jail was also going great. We had made a lot of progress with the women when it came to academics and most of them had cleared the exams we had organized in the previous month. The ones who couldn't were majorly disappointed, almost as if they had failed the biggest test of their lives. It was pretty terrible for us too because we didn't realize that failing in an examination would affect them this deeply; some of them stopped coming to class and the ones who came weren't enthusiastic about learning anymore. We hated knowing that they were upset since the purpose of the examination was only to determine who gets to study the next level in every subject and who needs to brush up the previous levels better. It was for their good and they didn't seem to have taken it too well. After two weeks of gloomy classroom atmosphere, I couldn't take it anymore and so Heena *ji* and I thought of an arrangement to make everyone happy without ruining our classroom structure. We decided to promote everyone so they would all be in the same class. That gave all the inmates much needed confidence. However, we divided them into different sections and since these sections were taught at a separate time by different people, we could work harder with the sections that had done poorly in the exams. Everyone was thrilled to be promoted and we realized that in a place like this, where everyone is speaking out his or her mind and heart all the time, healthy competition is just impossible.

Apart from teaching and handling the schoolwork in the Jail, I would often stay back after school hours just to interact with everyone. It was different from earlier insofar as now I had my sense of physical space and freedom. I knew I wasn't confined to that campus but surprisingly that worked for me when it came to interacting with the women. They opened up more and I got to know them better. Now I wasn't just another person listening to them speak, now I could actually help them with their problems. It was overwhelming to be in that Jail every time. I would go there twice a week and still every time I'd enter everyone and everything felt so warm. However, a strange feeling enveloped me whenever I entered that space. As if something was missing, something essential. The absence of that thing didn't make me feel complete. I always kept looking for something, though most of the times it wasn't at a conscious level. While teaching sometimes, when a child entered a room, my eyes would inevitably snap up, and my heartbeat would swiftly drop low for about a quarter of a second because I would mistake them for Kali. I would be disappointed every time. That feeling of my heart sinking every time this happened was a little heartbreaking. Everything was beautiful but that missing piece, that incomplete bit, always made me feel as if I was almost whole. That feeling was saddening because when you're aiming at something and you miss your goal by a tiny bit, it hurts way more than when you miss it by a huge margin.

I often went and sat with Aarti *ji* though. She was the only person who understood exactly how I felt and that's why talking to her always kept me going. She had become quite optimistic about life as opposed to how she was earlier when I was in Jail. It is funny how humans function. When she had Kali with her she would be worried all the time and had almost lost all hopes of a better life, and today when she didn't know where Kali was, she would calm me down and tell me things would be all right whenever I worried too much. She always told me how devastated she was when they first asked Kali to leave the Jail. She told me it was as if they were taking her lifeline away and she was almost certain she wouldn't survive without Kali because she was her only reason to live. However, she convinced Kali to leave the Jail happily because she knew it would be good for her, because she could do something out of her life. Aarti *ji* was willing to sacrifice everything for Kali's good. Although she expected loneliness to take over her life once Kali left, surprisingly that didn't happen and instead she felt a strange sense of peace. She always talked about peace and I could always hear my thoughts echo in her words. She told me how strange she felt when this peace within her didn't quiver when I informed her that Kali was missing. She was worried, obviously, but then she also knew she was doing way better than she had expected herself to do. My hopefulness about Kali came from this peace Aarti *ji* felt within her. And I think it was the other way round for her. We were both drawing from each other without realizing it much. One thing that we did know, however, was that this peace was Kali. And that made us sure that she was doing okay. It was as if we had both built a castle with playing cards, it looked magnificent but it was just about staying there, and anything, absolutely anything could have destroyed it completely.

"*Arre* Ayaana *ji*, I didn't see you standing there. Come sit." I went to see Aarti *ji* every time I came to the Jail even when it was just for a couple of minutes. She came for classes regularly but I wasn't teaching her anything myself.

"I was just waiting for you to complete the last bit of your stitching. It looks absolutely stunning!" I held the muffler she had made. It was perfectly knitted with just plain black thread.

"Look at it carefully Ayanna *ji*."

I was a little perplexed. I didn't quite understand what she wanted me to look at and so I started fiddling with the ends of the muffler until she turned it over and showed me the two little stars she had made on one corner.

"I made this one for you," and while saying that she wrapped the muffler around my neck.

I was speechless. I stood there thoughtless and motionless. Such was the power of these sudden and unexpected acts of immense love and warmth.

I embraced her and held onto her for sometime.

"Did you like it?" She asked me so innocently; I could almost feel like I was talking to Kali.

"Like? I don't know what to say Aarti *ji*. Why did you work so hard for me?"

"I wanted to do something for you. I don't think you know how significant you are. The comfort you bring along with you makes me want to keep going."

"It's the same for me. I hope I can bring Kali back to you someday."

"It's not even about that. I have met so many people in my life, some before I came here, and some in this place. All those people, each and every one of them was just passing by, they were strolling through my life. Not that some of those people weren't important to me, they surely were. They affected me and changed me in someway but then they were important to me just in that very moment and then they just walked by. But you, you nearly walked by, and then turned around and stayed. I don't know why, or maybe I do. But I just wanted to tell you that not many people do that, not many people have the courage to turn around and stay. You had the courage and that's why I wish for all your wishes to come true." She never really expressed how she felt about me before and although we both knew we were very special for each other, we never said it out loud. But today she did, and it was lyrical.

"I am glad I turned around Aarti *ji*. I am glad."

You know how you do things for others without waiting for recognition? When you just do things because you know it's the right thing to do. I never wanted Aarti *ji* or for that matter anybody else in the Jail to feel they owed me something, or to even realize that my life was shaped around them. However, today, when Aarti *ji* said what she said, I felt like everything, every little thing I had done, no matter how small, was worthwhile.

"Thank you again."

"Won't you ask me why did I choose to give this to you today?"

"Oh, I didn't think of that. Why today, Aarti *ji*?"

"They announced the result of my court hearing yesterday. I won Ayanna *ji*, we won."

We had arranged a lawyer to fight for Aarti *ji* a few months ago, but we had little hope for any positive turns since she had already confessed her crime in the court. However, we were fighting to lessen her term in jail because she killed her husband to protect her daughter and herself.

"We won? What do you mean? I couldn't attend yesterdays hearing but Heena *ji* told me things were still uncertain."

"Yes. But I don't know how, yesterday after the hearing I was called by the superintendent, he said I was free to leave."

"I don't believe this. I don't know what to say."

I hugged her with all my might, partly because I was happy she was going to get her freedom after all these years, and partly because I knew this Jail wouldn't be the same without her.

"Happy?" I asked her because I needed to know.

"I am not able to understand this Ayanna *ji*. All of a sudden I'll have a life beyond these four walls and I have no idea what it is going to be like. After all these years, I feel I'll be too lonely without Kali. I can start working in the parlor again but will I have something to look forward to then?"

"You will Aarti *ji*. There is always something to look forward to because no one knows what lies ahead."

"I am too scared. I have been confined for so long that the thought of being free scares me."

"I understand how you feel Aarti *ji*. But believe me, it is only going to get better after this."

"The world is too big Ayanna *ji*. How will I survive alone?"

"You won't be alone. I am there and so is Kali. I think you should stay with me"

"No Ayanna *ji*, I want to get back to my place, start afresh on my own, I want to feel worthy"

"You are more than that. Just remember I am always there"

"You won't forget me?"

I laughed at the impossibility of that situation and hugged her again.

"This is great news Aarti *ji*. It's time for me to leave, I'll get back and see where your case stands now and when can you actually leave this place. I'll come meet you again before you leave."

III

Weeks passed before Aarti *ji* could physically leave the jail. I say physically because mentally she was already free. It took her time to realize things and take in the news but once she did, she sparkled. Once she told me, "I had the same dream again last night Ayanna *ji*, but the beautiful part is that now I have the freedom to make it come true." I asked her what the dream was about? And she smiled and said, "being free."

I think more than anything, she knew she could go out and make an effort to actually find Kali on her own and put an end to the uncertainties. She had asked me to go to a few places to look for Kali but I couldn't find her there, maybe now she wanted to see those places herself just to make sure, just to be able to say to herself that she tried too.

I decided to go to the Jail on the day Aarti *ji* was supposed to leave. I wanted to make sure she faces no official issues, but more than that I wanted to be sure she doesn't get lost when she enters the world outside those four walls. We completed all the formalities and I drove her down to the place where she lived earlier. It was in a terrible condition but she told me it wasn't any better when she left it. We cleaned the tiny room quickly, after which I decided to leave. I hugged her and promised to come back soon.

IV

Days and months passed by and I never felt I was in the wrong place, doing something that I shouldn't be doing. There were phases when the results of our effort and hard work would take too much time to materialize but I had gotten used to this process by now. I had learnt how to remain calm while waiting and how to not equate hard work with positive results. To be honest, we would face disappointment more than success but it was all part of the cycle, a part of the small steps we were taking, which we knew were bringing us closer to where we wanted to be. However, we knew we were still very, very far away and reaching the destination was probably out of the question. The point was to never take a step backward, and none of us believed in doing that. It's strange how I felt so satisfied every single day, including the long days ending with disappointments, because I knew I was here, and I was trying, and nothing could stop me from doing so. I never waited for the results, for the right answers, for others to conform; I just wanted to make an effort, give it my best and hope it'll all work out. Of course, I reached this state after struggling with several breakdowns, but not even once did I feel I was in the wrong place, working hard for the wrong people. And that made everything fall in place every time.

V

I would meet Aarti *ji* once in a while, whenever I could take out the time from work. Initially of course, I would meet her more frequently because that is when I felt she needed me the most. After days of struggling with acceptance from society, which accused her of being a murderer, she learnt how to stay at peace without people's approval. She had learnt it a harsh way that life outside the Jail would never be the same for her. She took a lot of time to realize she shouldn't expect it to be the same, that she didn't need it to be the same. She wanted to resume working at the parlor where she had worked before going to Jail but the proprietors did not take her back. They thought she would add a bad reputation to the parlor and they would lose clients. I remember she broke down that day while talking to me.

"I was better off inside that Jail Ayanna *ji*. What do I do with the rest of my life now? I don't know how to deal with this situation. There is just nothingness all around. When I stepped out of that Jail I was so sure of myself, I just knew I could finally get things right. They sound so good when you think about them, talk about them, those words, the ones even you always speak about: hope, happiness and beauty. They are not meant for everyone Ayanna *ji*. Not everyone. They sound great but are actually very hollow when you begin to deal with this real life. I remained calm for so long, and I would be honest with you, I was truly at peace because I knew I was hoping but till when? When do I stop? You think now is the time? Or should I still be happy living this life? It is like nothing is moving, everything is just stuck in this moment and I cannot make it move, no matter how hard I try. It is frustrating Ayanna *ji*: to try and to fail, to hope and to be disappointed, every time, every single time. I don't know where my daughter is, what she is doing, what she looks like now, nothing at all. I just want to close my eyes sometimes and think of all this as a really terrible dream and wake up to feel a new day, a day which has something beautiful in it, something happy, something hopeful. Tell me Ayanna *ji*, say something, do something! Where is my Kali? Where is that hope?"

I had known Aarti *ji* for so long now, but never in so many years had she sounded so pessimistic, so dull and so weak. Even in the toughest of situations there was a strong side to her, which kept her going every time. I knew that day, that the only way to re-instill life in her was to rekindle that side of her, which I knew still existed somewhere within her.

"Remember that dream of yours you told me about? Where just the thought of being free made you so happy?" I asked her.

"I remember Ayanna *ji*, I was a fool. I thought I could do something worthwhile with my freedom. But it is so hard to resume, even if I want to, even if I try, every second there is something or someone just waiting to remind me that the world is not where I left it and that makes me an outcast. It's as if I don't belong outside those four walls. There is nobody and nothing."

"You will let people bring you down like this?" Seeing the glass as half full was only possible when there was something in the glass after all, I guess.

"What do I do?"

"Not this Aarti *ji*. You know you keep me going, you can't be like this."

"Don't you feel it sometimes too? Completely hopeless?"

"No, I haven't felt that way in a very long time. This is where I want to be, no matter how futile some of my efforts are, I know I am at least trying. It's a choice I am making Aarti *ji*."

"You are unbelievable."

"No, I am not. I am more ordinary than I have ever been. I don't even know what it is."

"At least you have a choice."

"Even you have one. I think everyone does."

"What is my choice?"

"Continue studying with the other girls at my office and I'll find you some work there."

"Those girls are so young Ayanna *ji*. I won't fit in."

"You don't have to. Who says fitting in is important or even relevant?"

"But.."

"See, this, this is what I am saying, you have a choice, you have a choice every second. We are all making choices every moment, we just don't realize it. You have to get up and dust off. I did too you know. You cannot be living like this. I won't let you live like this."

"I don't want you to do so much for me Ayanna *ji*. I will feel so indebted."

"What am I doing? I am offering you a job because I think you'll be able to do it; you'll be getting paid for it because you are working for it. What's my role in this?"

After some convincing she agreed to learn and work. She joined the other office of the NGO wherein she would assist people with their work and sometimes do minor chores in the office. I could see the change in her within days and it made me incredibly happy. Since both of us were working in different branches we would not see each other often. But when we met it was beautiful. Although most of our conversations still revolved around Kali, we now also spoke about work a little.

VI

My relationship with my parents had improved over time. In fact, in some ways, it had become better than how it used to be before I came to India for the first time. Adi had made me realize that not communicating the right feelings was the main cause of the misunderstandings between us. They were never able to understand me because I never expressed myself well. I would either not explain everything I felt completely, or just remain silent whenever they would question my decisions. My reasoning behind this was the assumption that they wouldn't understand me so I didn't want to try, but more importantly it was about my inability to express myself to anyone in general. However, the one thing that had changed in me while working with this organization was that I had learnt the art of communicating, of expressing myself, of telling people how I feel. This was partly because nobody at office believed in small talks, for instance they would never ask 'how are you' just for the sake of being social, so you had to always know how you were feeling and also how to explain that to someone. Adi's visit made me realize that my parents were very worried about me and that not talking to them about anything was just worsening the situation. Since I had complete faith in the decision I had taken, I had to make sure that they believed in me too. So from that day onward, I made sure I spoke to them, about the things they had a right to know. I talked about how much I wanted to be here and why this was so important to me. I also made sure I made them understand that my decision of coming to India and staying here hadn't, in anyway, lessened my love for them. I realized I had to express my love for them and not assume that they would know anyway. I had to make them a part of my life here, because even though I never stopped loving them, it did appear as if I had. Two months back I asked them to visit me, to spend their annual vacation in India instead, and so they came over to stay with me for a while. It was a beautiful time. Even though I couldn't travel around much with them, just seeing them and spending time with them after so long felt surreal. Making them meet everyone here, and showing them all the lovely places I spent my days at, made them understand my life in a better way. When they were leaving they asked me to stick to the path I had chosen, and they hugged me and told me they were proud of me. I cried a little then, it was as if someone had lifted a heavy weight from my body, I could float freely now, and I was even surer of the path I had chosen.

VII

I was getting ready for work when *maa* called.

"Hey *maa*, morning, I am just leaving home for work. I'll call you back from office?"

"You've received a mail from India. I have a feeling it is from Kali."

I stood still. I felt as if I was in vacuum. I could just hear the fading sound of a siren at a distance. I felt nothing, until I felt my eyes getting warm. I had to touch my face to realize I was crying, as if the tears came out from a very silent place deep inside me, so silent that the absence of sound could be heard, so deep that I felt infinite within.

"Ayanna, are you there?" I think I blanked out for a couple of minutes.

"*Maa*, please open it, please, tell me is it her?" I was shivering, and so was my voice.

"Okay, *beta*, wait."

"*Maa*, what if it is her, please tell me, *maa*..?"

"It is from Kali."

It is from Kali. That meant she was okay, she was somewhere, and probably I'll know soon where that somewhere was. In that moment all I wanted was someone to hold me and tell me this is real, but I would have believed that person only if that person was Kali. For a second, I was in a dream, a beautiful dream, and even though I did not know what that mail contained, I knew the wait was over and that Kali still remembered me. That second felt like that run from my classroom to the jailer's office when my parents came to take me away. Just that run, that thoughtless feeling of knowing the uncertainty is over.

"Are you okay darling?"

"What is it *maa*, what is in the mail, why aren't you speaking?"

"It is a letter and this, um, other thing, I think something she made for you. It is beautiful."

I just wanted her in front of me. I couldn't be where I was; I couldn't be where I was without her being there.

"It is a bird.. really colorful.. it has all the colors I can imagine," *Maa* said, and I smiled. Kali still loved colors, and she still remembers I love colors too.

"When did she send it *maa*? What is written in the letter? Tell me that? Was it a long time back? Has she written where she is? How is she doing? Tell me *maa*? Tell me all this?" I had snapped out of my dream and I needed to know the answers now and I hoped with all my might that the answers were the ones I had been waiting to hear. I hoped with all my strength that the answers lead me to her, not one or two steps closer but right where she was. I couldn't be composed after this, I just had to be there, be where she was. That was the only way I could have gotten over this feeling, this adrenaline.

"It just arrived *beta,* she sent it one week back. Wait, I'll just read it out to you."

"Dearest Ummi,

I know you are somewhere out there, loving me, and so I am writing to you again, hoping that I will hear from you this time, not because I want you to give up on your dreams and come meet me, but because I need to know if you're doing fine. It has been so long Ummi. I don't know why you did not reply to my first letter but I suppose I don't need to know. Never in all these years did I doubt your love for me even once. I feel you and Ammi around all the time… and I miss both of you dearly. I still believe in all that you taught me, I still believe in hope. I have so many things to tell you.

When they took me to the children's home, I knew that I had to be happy in that place, and I would have been happy as long as I got to learn, to read and to write. It was a bad place Ummi. So bad. They did not send us to school and spoke to us as if we were nothing. One day, one of the wardens caught me reading a book at night. It is true that I had picked up the book from the manager's office and I shouldn't have done that, but I didn't mean to steal it Ummi. I just wanted to read the book. It had the picture of an ocean on its cover page, how could I have resisted that book? I had to open it to see what the ocean looked like, what was inside it, how deep it was, how big it was. I found out that night that it is endless, you were right. But was this finding worth all the screaming and insulting I faced later on? They called me a thief and said they weren't surprised because I had my mom's blood running in my veins. I couldn't bear to hear all that Ummi. Ammi was right, you know she never meant to do any wrong, and you know how much she seeks for forgiveness from herself everyday. I didn't understand them, even though I tried to. They accused me of theft, but I didn't steal anything expensive, and I didn't steal money. I was just reading about the ocean. Why did they slap me for that? I thought about it for days Ummi, for days. The other children stopped talking to me because they thought of me as a thief; some of them started calling me 'chor' (thief) instead of Kali. I just couldn't take it. I cried a lot one night and missed you so much then. You would have understood me. Did I do anything wrong? I knew one thing, that I couldn't have stayed in that place for long, not because everyone looked at me as a thief, or because everyone hated me, but because there was no one to teach me, nobody wanted to give things away or share what they had, not even knowledge. Despite all this, I decided to stay for a while, because I had sent you that letter and I was very sure you would come and save me. I didn't know how long the letter would take to reach you or how long you would take to reach me, so I waited for long, till one day I had to leave. Why didn't you come Ummi? I am sure the letter did not reach you. Don't be sad about it, because I have never been unhappy because of you. You're still beautiful, and will always be.

I ran away from that place Ummi. I don't know whether I did the right thing or not but I couldn't have stayed there any longer. There was so much darkness in that place. I tried to find the light Ummi, because I know you would have asked me to do that, but I couldn't. I am sorry. I had to step out of that place. I was so scared that night, scared of everything, scared of what I was leaving behind and scared of where I was going. But I ran, hoping I was running the right way. I didn't have anything on me to survive, not even a single rupee. I think I was stupid back then to be thinking like this, but I think I coped, after days and nights of being terrified and being caught in the unknown, I finally saw the light.

I am not telling you all this because I want you to do something for me. I am telling you because I need to share this with someone who knows me, someone who will hear my story and understand it. Someone who will know I wasn't wrong or senseless, though most of the time I appeared to be. The hardest part about leaving that place was not being sure about whether you would come or not. I waited for one month thinking, what if she comes tomorrow, what if I miss her by a second in case I leave. The sad part was, I would have never known. I would have never found out whether you came the next second, or the next day. Did you?

I spent days and nights on the roads, without any food or money, until I made two friends: Minty and Ajay. I met them on the streets one night and they offered me food. They worked at a construction site around that area. Their job was to carry cement from one block to another and they would get paid for it on certain days if the manager was in a good mood, otherwise they would at least get food, which would keep them alive. They were so nice to me Ummi. They shared their food with me and asked me to stay on the construction site with them. They were so much fun. They would make me laugh all the time, even while working. They did not look down upon my mother or me when I told them about where I came from. They just laughed. Is laughing about everything good Ummi? I don't know, I felt so strange when they laughed after listening to my story but I laughed with them because I was happy it didn't change the way they looked at me. They would laugh all the time, even after someone scolded them. They taught me how to laugh whenever you can, whenever you feel like. It is a good lesson Ummi. Talking to them was so easy because they would make it sound so uncomplicated by laughing about it. The three of us faced everything together, be it days without food or those rare times when the wife of the owner brought great food for us. I spent some time working on the site. It was hard and tiring but it was fun because of Minty and Ajay. Friends are important no Ummi? Are you my friend too? I missed you so much all this while. I even told Minty and Ajay about you, they were very happy when I told them I could speak English. I taught them a few words too. It was fun.

One day the lady, who sometimes brought us food, asked all the children living on the construction site to meet her at a park nearby. I was very fond of her, especially because she would ruffle my hair exactly like you did whenever she gave me food. In fact, all the children really liked her and so all of us went to the park. She informed us how she was working for a community club and had decided to fund a child's education. She told us she would choose one of us working on the construction site because she was very fond of us. I was so happy when I heard that Ummi. I could have joined school again. That lady reminded me of you, and that was the best part about her. She said she would play some games with us and whoever performed the best in those games would be chosen to go to school. It was strange how some children left after hearing this. Why didn't they want to study Ummi? I wish they had stayed because I think the lady became a little sad when some of them left. I did not know back then whether I would win or not, but the games were a lot of fun. It felt nice to do something different that day. I won Ummi and I would thank you for that. Thank you for correcting me every time I said something wrong. Thank you for not giving up on me. It was such a happy day for me. I wish you and Ammi were there to share the happiness with me. You would have patted my back and kissed my forehead. I missed you terribly that day.

I joined school after two months of that workshop. That lady kept her promise. My wish came true. Is it because I wished too hard? Or is it because I deserved it? I don't know Ummi. The school I go to now is lovely. All the teachers speak in English so wonderfully. I had problems making friends in the beginning because I think people thought of me as a dirty kid but then slowly I made some friends. We are a group of three now and we always stay together. Minty and Ajay are still the same. Sometimes staying the same is the best thing. I still live with them. The lady who is funding my education, her name is Meghna. She visits me twice a month to see my progress, she tells me I am a bright child with beautiful eyes. I never told her about you until one day she saw me making this bird from plastic bags for my craft class. She asked me why was I making a bird, and I told her cause that's the only thing that can fly and reach you. After hearing everything about you, she told me she would send this bird to the address you gave me back then. She also cried a little. I don't know why? Is it sad Ummi? I don't know, but she is like an angel. She makes me really happy. I don't even know how to thank her. How can I? What can I do for her?

The bird I am sending along with this letter is for you. It is you. Colorful and free. That is exactly how you are no Ummi? I made sure I made it with all the colors I had. You still like all colors no? Because I still do. I want you to be like that bird. Fly. Fly in whichever direction you like, and one day fly to me too. Not now, not today, but whenever you miss me. I want to see your face again someday. I want to tell you what all I have learnt. I want to tell you how different the world outside those four walls is. It's not that nice, but there are certain things about it, which are so nice that they make up for all the bad things. It's funny how even a little light can brighten up a completely dark room? How having one good person can compensate for so many bad ones? How a little bit can sometimes be enough.

I worry about Ammi every single day. I don't know how she is and there is no way I can find out. I hope she is fine. I know she will take years to come out of the Jail, but the day she does, I want her to be proud of me. I want to give her all the happiness there is. I want to become capable enough to make her live a good life outside. I will be able to do that no Ummi? You think I can? I have faith in you and your answers. I look for you in my dreams sometimes and certain nights I do find you. I see you smiling at a distance, really far away, but your arms are always wide open, and I am running towards you. I never actually get to hold you though. I hope I will someday. It would be so wonderful.

I have learnt so much about the sky, the stars and moon in school. It's unbelievable. They are so far away from us and still shine so brightly. Do they even realize they are lighting up our world at night? They are like you. Do you realize you are lighting up my world from so far away Ummi? Am I still your Noor? I don't remember your face at all but I remember you so well. You said I'll grow up and childhood memories will fade, but they haven't. I don't know whether this letter will reach you or not, but if it does, my biggest wish will come true. Sometimes I feel the world is so big and that makes me feel so small. I wish I could see more of the world but there are so many places I'll never be able to see, so many things I'll never be able to learn. Why is it like that? Why are we so small as compared to the world? Doesn't it make you feel weak sometimes? A little powerless? To know there are so many things you can't reach, so many problems you can't solve, so many questions you just can't find answers to? The more I learn, the more I understand that not everything needs to be understood. Certain things are just meant to be complicated and you cannot simplify them. Do you agree Ummi? Do I still ask a lot of questions? My teachers like that about me but I sometimes think I shouldn't ask so many questions. I think it annoys other students. Should I not?

Meghna didi said that she would attach her address and phone number to this letter. This does not mean you have to come take me; I just need to know you are still there, that you actually happened. It has been so long that I have forgotten how you looked, though I remember thinking to myself back then that you are beautiful. I need to see your face because you are still a constant in my life, you are still my companion and that's why I need to know you are real and not something I made up in my dreams.

I love you Ummi, and I have missed you truly.

Always remember that you are that bird I made for you. You need to fly, because that is what you are meant to do. I hope your dreams have come true, but more than that I hope you are still dreaming.

I am sending you word again, I hope you are listening to me.

Love,
Noor."

My mother said that last word and then she couldn't speak anymore. It was as if she had tried really hard not to break down while reading it, so she broke down the minute she said the last word. She had just entered Kali's world and I wasn't surprised that she had been touched deeply too. It was Kali's enchantment.

I, on the other hand, had broken down long time back. Somewhere in between her story, her struggle, and her spirit I lost myself all over again. I had to find my way back because I could not have found her had I lost myself.

Everything around me lost meaning in that moment, and my only reality was this girl, this girl who spun my world around every time she entered it. It was magical. So surreal, and yet so real. I don't know what connected us or what kept us apart, but whatever it was I was grateful for it. It kept us attached even when we were apart physically. I wept because I could have protected Kali from all the pain she had to go through, but it was more because of the way she spoke about all her hardships: there was beauty in every word she wrote. I wept because the sufferings hadn't changed her soul. I wept because she still wanted me to dream, to fly and to come to her someday. I wept because I could embrace her again. Hold her so tight and never let go. I wept for I had finally got my answer. I wept because I could fulfill my promises now. I wept because I could prove Kali right. I wept because I could now complete my circle and feel whole.

I was still lost in her story when *maa* spoke, 'Ayanna, I understand what you have been struggling to make us understand all this while. I am sorry we didn't let you stay for those few hours in the Jail that day. I am sorry for not being able to know you."

"*Maa*, you all did more than enough for me."

"You can meet her now Ayanna. The wait is over."

The wait is over. I couldn't believe all this was actually happening. The only way I could have found out whether this dream-like morning was true or not was by seeing Kali in front of me. I took down the address and left my place to figure out whether I was living in a dream or living a dream.

PART 4

2015

"How did you know it was me Kali? You wrote that you didn't remember how I looked?" We were looking at the night sky again.

Although the day when my mother called to tell me about Kali's letter was a while ago, I still felt as if I was in a dream. It happened in the most unexpected manner, at a moment when I was not thinking about Kali. You know that feeling which takes over you almost completely? It is at the back of your mind every second of every day, so much so that that feeling becomes a part of your existence. However, there are these few moments, on certain days, when your mind is too occupied to realize that feeling exists? It was one of those moments when *maa* called that day. I was not missing Kali, even though Kali was always missing from me.

I found out where Kali was from Meghna. It was funny how one moment I did not even know that Meghna existed and the other moment she changed my life completely. She gave me that happiness I had been longing for. This one decision of hers to send that letter, to take a chance, made all the difference. Kali was right that there was no way to thank Meghna enough. I went to Kali's school to meet her that day. She stood in the playground with two of her friends. I immediately knew it was her. Even among thousands of children, I could recognize my Kali from a distance. She had grown. She wasn't the child anymore. Everything inside me felt so calm in that moment. No movement, just stillness. All of a sudden, she noticed me standing there, observing her. She ran towards me and embraced me. Just when I thought I had known all emotions there were, that moment happened, and all of a sudden I realized there was so much to this world I'd never know and so much within me I'd never be able to explore fully. The most beautiful feeling for me, however, was when I made Kali meet her mother. I could keep talking about how I felt then, but it will never be enough. Words will never do any justice to that feeling, so I'll keep that emotion to myself, untouched and pure, without altering it even a little by putting it in words.

"When I saw you standing there, I just remembered your face all of a sudden. I don't know how. I just knew it was you." She answered.

"Exactly like how I knew it was you?"

She laughed.

After a few minutes of silence she spoke again.

"*Ummi?*"

"Hmm?"

"Everything was so long ago but this time feels exactly the same, as if nothing has changed at all. How is this possible?"

"Maybe because we are looking at something that still looks exactly the same."

"But it isn't no?"

"What do you mean?"

"It looks the same but it is going through more changes than anything around us."

"That's the beauty of it I guess."

"What is the best thing you learnt over these years *Ummi*?"

"Giving."

She looked at me in a puzzled way.

"Most of us have one power Kali. It's the power to give. We keep collecting things for ourselves, piling them up, victory after victory, happiness after happiness, we make a huge heap of it and still feel incomplete. I learnt that giving is the soul of life. Giving whatever little we can, even if it's just a smile."

"What about you then?"

"Me? It keeps coming back to me. Every beautiful thing I give away comes back to me in some way or the other. Sometimes in an even more beautiful way."

"Really? How is that possible?"

"I don't know Kali. I really don't know how it works but what I know is that you need to have an eye to see the things when they are coming back to you."

"That's such a beautiful thing to learn."

"Learning is a funny process Kali. You never remember the exact moment when you actually learn something. It just happens. You don't really feel that moment when you just get something, understand something you had been struggling to understand for so long."

"I like learning."

I smiled.

"You wrote in your letter that you feel small compared to the universe."

"Don't you?"

"No, I don't. Why do you feel this way Kali?"

"It is so big *Ummi*. It doesn't end. Imagine you are a part of something that doesn't end. Isn't that scary *Ummi*? Doesn't that make you feel so little? As if you don't mean anything."

"Close your eyes Kali."

"Why?"

"I am trying to answer your question. You might want to hold my hand too."

She did as she was told.

"You're lying here with me. Close your eyes and see us lying here on this mattress on the terrace. Can you see us?"

"Yes *Ummi*, looks like that drawing I made for you."

"Brilliant. Now let's go a little further. Imagine us compared to the city."

I gave her a minute to picture it.

"Now as a part of the country."

She twitched her eyes and hesitated a bit.

"Go on Kali, think about it, let yourself imagine. I am holding your hand *Noor* and I promise I will not let you get lost."

She looked calm again.

"Think about us compared to all the continents now. Remember there are seven of them."

I paused for a while. It wasn't as easy to feel the moment completely. It was indeed an intimidating thought.

"What do you see Kali?"

"We are lying somewhere at the center of the earth."

"Good. Do you wish to go further?"

"I can barely see us *Ummi*. We are becoming smaller."

"Yes I know. Imagine us on the earth and compare the earth to all the other planets, the sun, the moons, and the stars, everything that exists in the universe. Compare us to the endless Kali. Compare us to infinity."

She tightened the grip of our hands then and I just knew she was doing it the right way. I needed to hold her hand as much as she needed to.

"What do you see?"

"I don't see us anymore. Hardly. We are there just because I am trying hard to see us, but we are actually not even there. We are so insignificant compared to infinity."

"How do you feel?"

"Scared"

"Why is that?"

"I am nothing *Ummi*. I can't see us anymore. Doesn't that make you feel powerless?"

"No."

"How come *Ummi*?"

"Open your eyes Kali."

She did as she was told.

"Why didn't it make you feel small *Ummi*?"

"Because in that moment infinity was within you and me"

She looked at me with the grey in her eyes and smiled, and I knew she had found her answers, exactly like I had found my whole.